Imperium

Imperium

A FICTION OF THE SOUTH SEAS

~~~~~

Christian Kracht

TRANSLATED FROM THE GERMAN BY DANIEL BOWLES

FARRAR, STRAUS AND GIROUX   NEW YORK

Farrar, Straus and Giroux
18 West 18th Street, New York 10011

Library of Congress Cataloging-in-Publication Data
Kracht, Christian, 1966–
    [Imperium. English]
    Imperium : a fiction of the South Seas / Christian Kracht ;
translated from the German by Daniel Bowles. — First edition.
        pages   cm
    ISBN 978-0-374-17524-5 (hardcover) — ISBN 978-0-374-70986-0
(e-book)
    1. Engelhardt, August, 1877–1919—Fiction.   2. Germany—
Colonies—Oceania—Fiction.   I. Bowles, Daniel, translator.   II. Title.

PT2671.R225 I5713 2015
833'.92—dc23

                                        2014039370

Designed by Jonathan D. Lippincott

Farrar, Straus and Giroux books may be purchased for educational,
business, or promotional use. For information on bulk purchases,
please contact the Macmillan Corporate and Premium Sales
Department at 1-800-221-7945, extension 5442, or write
to specialmarkets@macmillan.com.

www.fsgbooks.com
www.twitter.com/fsgbooks • www.facebook.com/fsgbooks

1   3   5   7   9   10   8   6   4   2

For Hope

Grave et religieux il reprend sa calme attitude:
il demeure—symbole qui grandit—et, penché
sur l'apparence du Monde, sent vaguement en lui,
résorbées, les générations humaines qui passent.

—André Gide

Naked people have little or no influence on society.

—Mark Twain

Part One

I

Beneath the long white clouds, beneath the resplendent sun, beneath the pale firmament could be heard, first, a prolonged tooting; then the ship's bell emphatically sounded the midday hour, and a Malaysian boy strode, gentle-footed and quiet, the length of the upper deck so as to wake with a circumspect squeeze of the shoulder those passengers who had drifted off to sleep again just after their lavish breakfast. Each morning, if one were traveling first class, Norddeutscher Lloyd, may God curse it, provided, through the skill of long-queued Chinese cooks, glorious Alphonso mangoes from Ceylon sliced open lengthwise and arranged artfully, fried eggs with bacon, along with chicken breast in a spicy marinade, prawns, aromatic rice, and a bold English porter beer. The very indulgence in the latter among those planters returning home, who—dressed in the white flannel of their guild—had slumped down onto the steamer chairs of the upper deck to sleep rather than retreating decorously to their beds, made for an exceedingly boorish, almost slovenly sight. The buttons of their trousers, open at the fly, dangled loosely; sauce stains from saffron-yellow curries coated their vests. It was altogether insufferable. Sallow, bristly, vulgar Germans, resembling aardvarks, were lying there and waking slowly from their digestive naps: Germans at the global zenith of their influence.

Thus, or roughly so, ran the thoughts of young August Engelhardt as he crossed his thin legs, wiping a few imagined crumbs from his garb with the back of his hand and gazing out grimly over the bulwarks onto the oily, smooth sea. Frigate birds escorted the ship on the right and left; it was never farther from shore than a hundred nautical miles. Up and down they dove, these great, swallowtail-like hunters whose consummate play at flight and curious preying maneuvers every sailor in the South Seas loved. Engelhardt himself was enchanted by the birds of the Pacific Ocean, particularly by the New Zealand bellbird, *Anthornis melanura*. Once, as a boy, he had pored over them for hours upon hours in the folios, had studied them and their glorious, sweeping plumage, which shimmered in the blazing sun of his childhood imagination, tracing their beaks, their colorful feathers, with his little fingers. But now, as Engelhardt sailed under their flapping wings, he no longer had eyes for them, only for the burly planters who, having carried within themselves untreated tertiary syphilis for quite some time, were now returning to their plantations and had fallen asleep over the dryly and tediously written articles in the *Tropenpflanzer* or the *Deutsche Kolonialzeitung*, smacking their lips while dreaming of bare-breasted, dusky Negro girls.

The word *planter* didn't quite capture it, for this term presupposed dignity, a knowledgeable engagement with both nature and the august miracle of growth; nay, one had to speak of *custodians* in the literal sense, for they were precisely that:

custodians of putative progress, these Philistines with their trimmed mustaches, styled in the fashion of Berlin or Munich from three years ago, beneath spider-veined nostrils that, for their part, quivered with every exhalation, and fluttering, spongy lips underneath, from which bubbles of spittle hung as if they would drift off into the breeze of their own accord, could they be but liberated from their labial adherence, like floating soap bubbles from a child's game.

The planters, in turn, peeped out from under their eyelids and saw sitting there, a bit off to the side, a trembling, barely twenty-five-year-old bundle of nerves with the melancholy eyes of a salamander, thin, slight, long-haired, wearing a shapeless ecru robe, with a long beard, the end of which swept uneasily over the collarless tunic, and they perhaps wondered for a moment about the significance of this man who at every other breakfast, indeed at every lunch, sat in a corner of the second-class salon alone at a table with a glass of juice before him, studiously dissecting one-half of a tropical fruit, then for dessert opening a paper package from which he spooned into a water glass some brown, powdery dust that by all indications consisted of pulverized soil. And then proceeded to eat this very dirt pudding! How eccentric! Most probably a preacher, clearly anemic, unsuited to life. But still essentially uninteresting. And especially futile to give further thought to the matter. Mentally, one gave him a year in the Pacific, shook one's head, closed one's eyelids, and fell back asleep mumbling incomprehensibly.

Those distinctly audible, creaking snores accompanied the German ship past the American Philippines, through the Strait of Luzon (there was no approaching Manila, because it was uncertain whether the war that had gripped the colony would still turn out well), through the waters of what seemed to be the infinitely large territory of the Dutch East Indies, and ultimately into the protectorate itself.

No, how he detested them. No, no, a thousand times no. Engelhardt opened and closed and reopened Schlickeysen's standard work *Fruit and Bread*, tried in vain to read a few paragraphs, and, with the stump of a pencil he perpetually carried with him in the pocket of his robe, jotted on the margin of a page a few notes that he himself could no longer decipher a moment later, despite having only just written them.

The ship rolled along calmly under a cloudless sky. At one point Engelhardt saw a pod of dolphins in the distance, but no sooner had he borrowed a pair of binoculars from the shipmaster than they had already plunged again into the unfathomable depths of the sea. Presently, the trim isle of Palau was reached, the mail sacks were delivered, and the island was left behind. At the next brief stop, in Yap, several outrigger canoes approached the great ship haltingly; there were offerings of half pigs and yams for sale, but neither the passengers nor the crew showed even the slightest interest in the peddled wares. Meanwhile, a canoe, while veering around, was seized by the eddy of the screws and pushed against the ship's side. The islander saved himself with a leap into the water, but the canoe split in twain, and the provisions, only moments ago raised aloft by brown hands toward the skies, now rolled about in the frothing water, and Engelhardt, leaning out far over the railing and looking down, clutching Schlickeysen's book with one hand, shuddered at the sight of a half pig that first floated, festooned with still-bleeding sinews on its flank, then sank down slowly into the indigo-blue ocean deep.

The *Prinz Waldemar* was a robust modern steamship of three thousand tons that traversed the Pacific Ocean toward Sydney, departing every twelve weeks from Hong Kong, and from there approached the German protectorate known as New Pomerania, then the Gazelle Peninsula, the new capital Herbertshöhe in Blanche Bay (and in that very place one of its two landing piers), whose easily navigable basin had been designated, in a fit of optimism, as a harbor.

Herbertshöhe was not Singapore; it essentially consisted of those two wooden jetties and a few intersecting broad boulevards where the trading posts of Forsayth, of Hernsheim & Company, and of Burns Philp had been erected, which, depending on one's point of view, might be regarded as rather impressive or less so. Then there was another fairly large building, that of the Jaluit Society, which traded guano in Yap and Palau, a police station, a church and its thoroughly picturesque cemetery, the Hotel Fürst Bismarck, the rival Hotel Deutscher Hof, a harbormaster's office, two or three taverns, a Chinatown hardly worth mentioning, a German Club, a small clinic under the provident supervision of Doctors Wind and Hagen, and the office of the governor, slightly elevated above the city on a hill covered in green grass that shone in the afternoon with an otherworldly gleam. But it was an up-and-coming, orderly, German town, and if one referred to it as a *backwater*, then it was only in ridicule, or because it rained so heavily that one couldn't make out anything at all thirty feet ahead.

After the downpours at midday the sun invariably shone, at three o'clock sharp, and in the chiaroscuro of the tall grass gloriously multicolored birds paraded about and preened their dripping plumage. Then, in the puddles of the avenues, beneath the coconut palms soaring high above, the native islander children romped about, barefoot, naked, many of them in short tattered pants (more holes than fabric); their crowns were graced by woolly hair that, through some curious whim of nature, was blond. They called Herbertshöhe Kokopo, which sounded much better and above all was more beautiful to say.

The German protectorates in the Pacific Ocean were without exception, in contrast to the African possessions of His Majesty Emperor Wilhelm II, completely superfluous. In this the experts agreed. The yield of copra, guano, and mother-of-pearl was far too inadequate to maintain so large an empire sprinkled around the infinitude of the Pacific Ocean. In distant Berlin, however, they spoke of the islands as precious gleaming pearls, strung along the chain of a necklace. Advocates and adversaries of the Pacific colonies could be found in droves, though it was primarily the still-nascent Social Democrats who most loudly questioned the relevance of the holdings in the South Seas.

Now, it is into this time that our chronicle falls, and if one wishes to narrate it, then one must bear in mind the future as well, for this account takes place at the very beginning of the twentieth century, which until just before the midpoint of its duration looked as if it would become the Century of the Germans, the century in which Germany would take its rightful place of honor and precedence at the table of nations, and from the perch of that new century, aged but a few years according to the lives of men, this appeared to be precisely the case. Thus, as a stand-in, the tale of but a single German will now be told, of a romantic who was, as are so many of this species, a thwarted artist; and if at times, in the course of things, parallels arise with a later German romantic and vegetarian who perhaps ought to have remained at his easel, then this is entirely intentional and naturally, do pardon, consistent *in nuce*. At the moment, the latter is still just a pimply, cranky lad who gets innumerable smacks from his father. Just wait and see, though: he grows and grows.

And so, on board the *Prinz Waldemar* we find the young August Engelhardt from Nuremberg: beard-wearer, vegetarian, nudist. Some time ago he had published in Germany a book with the enthusiastic title *A Carefree Future*; now he was traveling to New Pomerania to purchase land for a coconut plantation—how much exactly and where, he did not yet know. He was to become a planter—not out of greed for profit, but out of a deeply held belief that he could change forever, by the force of his grand idea, this world that seemed to him so cruel, stupid, and horrible.

After having adjudged all other foodstuffs unclean by process of elimination, Engelhardt had abruptly stumbled upon the fruit of the coconut palm. No other possibility existed; *Cocos nucifera* was, as Engelhardt had realized on his own, the proverbial crown of creation; it was the fruit of Yggdrasil, world-tree. It grew at the highest point of the palm, facing the sun and our luminous lord God; it gave us water, milk, coconut oil, and nutritious pulp; unique in nature, it provided humankind with the element selenium; from its fibers one wove mats, roofs, and ropes; from its trunk one built furniture and entire houses; from its pit one produced oil to drive away the darkness and to anoint the skin; even the hollowed-out, empty shell made an excellent vessel from which one could manufacture bowls, spoons, tankards, indeed even buttons; burning the empty shell, finally, was not only far superior to burning traditional firewood, but was also an excellent means of keeping away mosquitoes and flies with its smoke; in short, the coconut was perfect. Whosoever subsisted solely on it would become godly, would become immortal. August Engelhardt's most fervent wish, his destiny in fact, was to establish a colony of cocovores. He viewed himself at once as a prophet and a missionary. For this reason did he sail to the South Seas, which had lured infinitely many dreamers with its siren song of paradise.

Beneath its belching smokestack, the *Prinz Waldemar* maintained its ramrod-straight course toward Herbertshöhe. And while great tubs of leftover food were dumped twice daily into the sea from the quarterdeck, to the south the dark coast of Kaiser-Wilhelmsland drew past, the Finisterre Range, as Engelhardt's map had read forebodingly, and the unexplored, dangerous lands that lay beyond, where no German had yet set foot. One hundred thousand million coconut palms were growing there. Engelhardt had not been at all prepared for the almost painful beauty of this southern sea; sunbeams pierced the clouds in luminous shafts, and every evening peaceful mildness descended upon the coastlines and their terraced mountain chains, which extended, one after the other, into infinity in the sugary purple light of dusk.

A gentleman in a white tropical suit and pince-nez approached him, one who though corpulent did not seem quite as obtuse as his colleagues, and Engelhardt was momentarily seized by that almost pathological shyness that always possessed him whenever he met people who were completely convinced of the justness of their actions and existence. Did

Engelhardt know what the recliner was called in which he and the other passengers dozed away their afternoons on deck? Engelhardt said no without a word, lowering his head to express his intention of immersing himself again in Schlick-eysen, but the planter who was now introducing himself with a minuscule bow as Mr. Hartmut Otto came another step closer, as if he needed to confide an exceptionally important secret. Because of its extendable wooden leg rests, the deck chair was called, Engelhardt ought to sit down for this, please, the *Bombay fornicator.*

Engelhardt didn't quite understand and, moreover, found labored jokes of a carnal nature coarse, though he considered the sexual act something wholly natural, something absolutely ordained by God, not a part of a repressed, falsely understood manly discipline. He refrained from mentioning this, however, but gave the planter a somewhat baffled and scrutinizing look. Now it was up to Mr. Otto, as it were, to backpedal and, with a rapid succession of wiping hand gestures, to enumerate his dealings in the German protectorate. Let's forget it, he said, taking a seat on the lower part of the recliner with aplomb while loosening his shirt collar, which had grown slightly damp from humidity and perspiration. He was, he reported while artfully twirling the ends of his mustachio skyward with his fingers, on the hunt for *Paradisaeidae,* birds of paradise, whose feathers, Otto ought to know, currently fetched *astronomical* prices in the drawing rooms of the New World, from New York to Buenos Aires. Did the birds have to lose their lives in the process? Engelhardt now wanted to know, for he saw that Otto had made himself comfortable, leaving no further possibility of undertaking evasive action toward his book. Ideally, *nota bene,* the plumes were harvested from the animals while they were alive—certainly there were traders who'd merely have gathered up those decorative adornments that had fallen out onto the jungle floor from the rump of mature birds of paradise; but he, Otto, put no stock in such methods. Rather, the plumes must display traces of blood at the lower end of the quill, as a seal of quality, so to speak, and if they did not, he wouldn't buy them. Engelhardt grimaced—he easily became queasy—then the midday bell was ringing, and Otto took hold of his arm gently and firmly; but now he really must do him the honor of dining with him.

Hartmut Otto was a moral person in the actual meaning of the term, even if his civility had sprung from the preceding century and he couldn't muster much understanding for the new age now dawning, the protagonist of which would be August Engelhardt. To be sure, the bird hunter had read progressive scientists, like Alfred Russel Wallace, Lamarck, and Darwin, indeed with a certain meticulousness, especially their taxonomic essays, but he not only lacked faith in modernity as a cumulative process; he was also incapable of recognizing and accepting a radical spirit (as Wallace and Darwin had been, for instance), should he encounter him in person, perchance on a sea voyage, as he had just now. Engelhardt's vegetarianism, as we shall soon see, was anathema enough to Otto.

Engelhardt begrudgingly allowed himself to be led to dine in the first-class salon. There—where one sat in heavy neo-Gothic chairs, the seat backs of which were stuffed with horsehair, while resting one's gaze on gilt-framed reproductions of Dutch masters—upon Otto's signal to the Malaysian steward, he was served, quite contrary to Engelhardt's usual daily eating habits, a plate of steaming spaetzle and a pork chop with a sumptuous brown gravy. Engelhardt looked with bald revulsion upon the piece of meat sitting there before him in its bed of noodles, its edges an iridescent blue.

Otto, who was essentially a good-natured man, thought his counterpart was probably intimidated, since Engelhardt, as a second-class passenger, didn't know how he would pay for what was for him an extravagant midday repast, and he invited him to eat of the pork chop, yes, by all means, please, it was his treat, to which Engelhardt, politely but with the firmness of his (and Schopenhauer's, and Emerson's) conscience replied, no, thank you, he was an avowed vegetarian in general and a frugivore in particular, and might he perhaps request a green salad, not dressed, without salt and pepper.

The bird dealer paused, replaced the knife and fork he had already been holding over his plate to its right and left, chuckled, dabbed at his upper lip and mustachio with his napkin, and then burst into a barking, bleating, even snorting fit of laughter. Tears sprang from his eyes. First his napkin sailed to the floor, then a plate shattered, and all the while Otto repeated the words *salad* and *frugivore* again and again, turning a purplish red as if he were about to asphyxiate. While those at the neighboring table leapt up to rid him, with sweeping blows to the back, of what they supposed was a piece of bone lodged in his trachea, August Engelhardt sat across from him looking at the floor, waggling the sandal laced to his left ankle with manic swiftness. A Chinese cook came running from the galley, a dripping whisk still in his hand.

Two parties formed and began to argue most vigorously. Engelhardt heard a few bits clearly amid the tumult; they concerned his, Engelhardt's, right to refuse the consumption of meat. What's more, they spoke of savages—if one may even still call them that, said one of the plantation owners. Had things gotten so bad now that a German in the protectorate was no longer permitted to distinguish a wog from a Rhinelander? Yet we ought to be happy, another said, to have vegetable products listed on the menu, especially as large parts of our merry island empire have long since returned to anthropophagy after we so arduously weaned the savages off it with Draconian measures. *Oh, nonsense! Old hat!* came the opposing shout. And yet, and yet—only four months ago they ate a padre over on Tumleo among the Steyler Missionary Sisters. The body parts of the man of God that weren't consumed immediately were pickled, shipped up the coast, and sold in the Dutch East Indies.

Engelhardt's sense of shame threatened to overwhelm him. He went pale, then red, and made moves to rise and quit this contemptuous salon. He smoothed the napkin before him on the table and gave his thanks to Hartmut Otto quietly, almost inaudibly, without a trace of irony. His thin upper arm seized rudely by a plantation owner seeking to prevent him from leaving, he nevertheless managed to pry himself free with a brusque jerk of his shoulders, traversed the room in a few paces, and opened the salon door leading directly out on deck. There he paused, agitated, and wiped his forehead with the back of his hand. And while he inhaled the muggy tropical air and exhaled it again, pondering whether he ought not perhaps cling to the wall of the promenade deck only to discard this thought immediately as sissy, a deep, deep loneliness, far more unfathomable than he had ever felt it in his native Franconia, finally took possession of him. He had ended up here among horrible people, among loveless, crude barbarians.

He slept poorly that night. A long way off, a thunderstorm drew past the *Prinz Waldemar*, and the erratic convulsions of sheet lightning, following some random rhythm, plunged the steamship again and again into a ghostly, pallid snow-white. While tossing and turning in his clammy sheets, glimpsing above him on the ceiling in half-awake moments of fright, oddly enough, the contours of England, he finally fell into a deeper sleep—the storm could still be heard only as very distant, deep rumbling—and dreamed of a cultic temple, erected beneath the faintly shining evening sun upon the beach of a windless Baltic Sea, illuminated by Viking torches stuck in the sand. A burial was taking place there; stalwart Norsemen stood watch at the temple, children whose blond hair had been braided into wreaths played quietly at their feet on flutes of bone, the raft on which the dead man lay in repose was shoved out to sea in the gloaming, and a giant of a man, standing up to his waist in the water, ignited the kindling, after which it drifted, slowly and mournfully, gradually catching fire, northward toward Hyperborea.

Early the next morning, as the steamship sailed into Blanche Bay amid glistening sunlight, merry band music, and the loud tooting of her siren, Engelhardt was standing at the bulwarks, slightly disheveled, still sensing in his bones that wondrous, uncanny dream from the night before, the content of which was becoming ever more nebulous the closer they got to land. It is likely he suspected that the two ships, the modern steamship and the pagan burial raft, were entangled with one another in meaning and significance; yet this morning he found himself not at all in the mood to draw conclusions from that dream about his own departure from home, which, while not hasty, had, quite embarrassingly, borne the seal of cudgeling Prussian police brutality. Well, he thought, he wasn't going to die here on these green shores.

Sensing within himself an almost feline readiness to pounce, he observed all aflutter the approaching dry land. So this was it, his Zion. Here in this terra incognita he would settle, from this spot on the globe his presence would be projected. He ran upstairs and down, aquiver, turned around again abruptly upon reaching the quarterdeck, where several gentlemen who were inebriated yet again at breakfast—the vile bird dealer Otto was not among them—had raised their glasses and shouted to him cheerfully that he ought to let bygones be bygones, they wished to be friends again, and after all, one must stick together among Germans in the protectorate, et cetera. Ignoring these louts, he surveyed the stately sweep of the coastline, keeping watch for inlets, irregularities, elevations.

Palms as tall as houses thrust upward from the steaming bush of New Pomerania. Blue haze rose from the wooded slopes; here and there one could make out glades, and in them solitary grass huts. A macaque shrieked wretchedly. A gathering gray cloud front briefly blocked the sun and then let it shine forth once more. Engelhardt's fingers drummed one or two impatient marches; again the tooting ship's siren sounded. The cone of a volcano only half covered by trees pushed its way into view. All of a sudden red droplets spattered onto the white-painted balustrade, and he was seized with fright. It was blood dripping from his nose, and he had to race belowdecks, groping his way carefully down the ladders into the diffuse light of the steel corridors, lie on his back in his cabin's berth, and, with closed, throbbing eyelids, press a slowly reddening bedsheet over his face. From a jug covered by a towel he poured himself some fruit juice into a glass and drank it down in thirsty gulps.

Meanwhile, all of Herbertshöhe had gathered; it was the first week of September. They stood on wooden gangplanks, freshly combed, shaven, and furnished with new collars, awaiting what were no longer the most recent newspapers from Berlin; the beer that would remain iced now only a short while, and which was uncapped immediately—the first cases were hardly unloaded—and passed around bottle by bottle; the dozens of letters from home; and of course the newcomers: soldiers of fortune and adventurers, returning planters, the occasional researchers, ornithologists, and mineralogists, the destitute noblemen chased away from their impounded estates, the crazies, the flotsam and jetsam of the German Empire.

Engelhardt was standing in his cabin, at the porthole of the emptying steamship, to be precise, looking out through the double-paned glass onto Herbertshöhe. The nosebleed had ceased as suddenly as it had begun. He wasn't secure in his footing and leaned against the bulkhead of his cabin somewhat stooped, his cheek grazing the gauzy curtain fabric; in the pocket of his robe, he clasped the pencil stump with the fingers of his right hand. The sun shone through the porthole with tremendous strength. When the wispy cloth of the curtain touched him once more, he began to cry. He was overcome, his knees quaked, he felt as if the very last drop of his bravery had been sucked from his bones by means of some kind of contraption, and now the scaffolding that had once been held together solely by the glue of courage was buckling.

II

It was in Port Said, half an eternity ago (in reality just a few weeks earlier)—when his eleven overseas crates with one thousand two hundred books had been mistakenly unloaded and he fancied them lost, never to be seen again—that he had last wept, one or two almost saltless tears, out of desperation and the vague feeling that for the first time his courage was now truly failing him. After searching in vain for the harbormaster, he used his time to post to a good friend in Frankfurt a letter that he had written while still in the Mediterranean—he had wrapped it in a cotton cloth to protect it from the damp—and drank unsweetened peppermint tea on the terrace at Simon Arzt's for an hour and a half while a silent Nubian, with a white napkin, dried glasses that refracted the shimmering canal in the dazzling desert light.

All of Thoreau, Tolstoy, Stirner, Lamarck, Hobbes, Swedenborg, too, Madame Blavatsky and the theosophists—everything gone, everything lost. Alas, perhaps it was better this way, all that pointless thought, poof, shipped off somewhere else. Sullen, he made his way again to the pier and to his ship to Ceylon.

The idea occurred to him that one ought to hand out a few piasters among the stevedores, so Engelhardt dug into his tunic pockets and addressed a seaman whose ethnicity (Greek? Portuguese? Mexican? Armenian?) was indecipherable due to a regrettable one-sided facial paralysis. He gave him the money and heard the man fold the bills together while smacking his lips. But, but, please, effendi, his books were over there! They apologized to him and without further ado loaded the crates on board again; it had been a misunderstanding, they had made a silly mistake, supposing Herbertshöhe to be somewhere else, on the coast of German East Africa. Engelhardt's letter to his friend, wherein he wrote of *contamination by Europe* and of *the Garden of Eden*, turned up, insufficiently stamped, in the office of Port Said's French postal service; there it was laid aside, ultimately, to its eternal rest. In a receptacle for such envelopes, underneath a table, it gathered dust and was buried by other letters. After many years, the course of which spanned one or two world wars, it was baled and strung together with others in a hefty bundle by a Coptic wastepaper merchant and chauffeured in a donkey cart out to a squalid hut at the fringes of the Sinai Desert—which, however, Engelhardt, whose ship was sailing to Ceylon that very evening with him and his book crates aboard, was never to discover.

In Colombo, there were two luxurious grand hotels: the Galle Face, situated on the edge of a large maidan, and the Mount Lavinia, erected on a hill somewhat outside of and to the south of the city. Engelhardt, who would otherwise have certainly headed to more modest lodgings, had decided that he should indulge himself for once in Ceylon, and boarded a rickshaw after giving a liveried boy several annas, so that he might look after the whereabouts and custody of his baggage, which it had been necessary, yet again, to unload from the ship and store at the harbor. He made himself comfortable on the extraordinarily wide seat and wished to be conveyed to the Galle Face Hotel at a leisurely pace. But it went too quickly! The bare feet of the little old Ceylonese man slapped onomatopoeically and monotonously on the street before and below him; Engelhardt wondered whether the rickshaw wallah was running so fast because the asphalt was so hot, or whether the velocity was, so to speak, one of the expectations of passengers who wanted to arrive at their destination rapidly. He leaned down to touch the little man on the shoulder and communicate to him that he need not hurry so on his account, please, but the fellow did not understand him and even accelerated his pace, which is why, after finally arriving in front of the grand hotel, he collapsed beside the rickshaw, drenched in sweat and gasping for breath.

The liveried porter, a burly Sikh with a magnificent white beard, came running, blanketed the poor rickshaw wallah with reproachful curses, took Engelhardt's hand luggage from him with dozens of apologies, and, tossing a coin at the feet of the poor old man lying in the street, steered our friend into the cool and cavernous reception hall, where, with a practiced movement of his flattened hand, he rang a silver bell that had been affixed to the reception desk for this very purpose.

Engelhardt slept long and dreamlessly in a large white room. A modern electric fan hummed on the ceiling above him; now and again a gecko somewhere in the room chirped its bleating courtship song and then shot its tongue at a bug it had been approaching slyly, millimeter by millimeter. Around four in the morning, the window shutters rattled, a wind sprang up, and it rained for an hour. But Engelhardt heard nothing. Lying on his back, profoundly at ease, he slumbered away on the freshly starched sheets, hands folded on his chest. His long hair, liberated before bedtime from the practical hair band that tied it back during the day, encircled the head resting on the white pillow in dark blond waves as if he were Wagner's sleeping young Siegfried.

On the following day, in the compartment of the awfully sluggish train to Kandy, on the way to the old royal city of Ceylon, a Tamil gentleman sat opposite to him; his blue-black skin stood in peculiar contrast to the snow-white tufts of hair that jutted out from his ears as if they were woolly cauliflower rosettes attached to his head, right and left. The soporifically slow journey wound through shady coconut groves and emerald rice paddies. The gentleman wore a black suit and a high white collar that lent him the dignity of a magistrate or a state solicitor. Engelhardt was reading an amusing book (Dickens) as one switchback after another passed before the window and the view looked out onto gently sloping fields of tea—tea that grew in walkable furrows, from which protruded colorfully dressed, dark-skinned tea-picking women, green-filled baskets on their backs.

The gentleman had addressed him with a question, and Engelhardt, holding the page of the book he had just read with a wetted thumb and forefinger, asked him politely to repeat it, as the gentleman's English was accented with a melody and tonality so foreign that Engelhardt would have better understood an Australian, even a Texan, but this venerable Tamil? Almost not at all. While the afternoon dust danced through the open train window, they conversed as well as they were able—they had made an agreement to employ the idiom both used purely as a mediating language deliberately and slowly—about the relics of the Holy Lord Buddha and, in particular, for Engelhardt soon steered the conversation in that direction, about the coconut.

With soft gestures, the gentleman declared that, as a Tamil, he was beholden to Hinduism, but according to the sacred text of the Bhagavata Purana, the Buddha was one of the avatars of Vishnu, the twenty-fourth, to be precise, and for that reason—and here he introduced himself briskly as Mr. K. V. Govindarajan with a handshake that Engelhardt found pleasantly dry and firm—he was on the way to Kandy to view the tooth of the Buddha that was venerated there in a temple shrine. The relic at issue was the *dens caninus*, the upper left eyetooth. Govindarajan daintily raised a lip with the tip of his dark ring finger and graphically pointed out the location of the tooth in question; Engelhardt peered into the bone-white dentition embedded in perfectly healthy pink gums and mentally shuddered with a sensation of warm contentedness. His interlocutor's plain, unhurried, and yet touchingly emotive means of expression filled him with an intense feeling of sudden intimacy.

All at once, he reached for Govindarajan's hand and asked him outright whether he was a vegetarian. But of course, certainly, came the answer, he himself and his family had been subsisting for years on fruits alone. Engelhardt was scarcely capable of grasping the coincidence of this encounter. Across from him in the compartment sat not only a brother in spirit, a like-minded soul, but a man whose subsistence placed him on par with God. Were not the dark races centuries ahead of the white race? And didn't Hinduism, the highest expression of which was vegetarianism, i.e., love, constitute a force in the fabric of the universe, wouldn't its all-encompassing, lucid rustlings one day outshine like a blinding comet those nations upon which Christianity had bestowed a charitable love that excluded animals from its purview? Hadn't Rousseau and Burnett, following the vegetarian Plutarch, and as an overdue response to Hobbes's *Leviathan*, claimed that the primordial instinct inherent in mankind was the renunciation of meat? And hadn't Engelhardt's dreadful Uncle Kuno tried to make the consumption of ham more palatable to him as a young boy by rolling a pink cigar for him from the thin flaps of pig meat as he laughed and smirked, then sticking it into his young mouth, and holding a match to the protruding end, just for the fun of it? And, finally, wasn't the killing of animals, which is to say the preparation of meat and the nourishment of man with animal substances, really the preliminary stage of anthropophagy?

Engelhardt's knowledge of English was sometimes not entirely sufficient to formulate such questions exactly—and yet they had to come out; where he lacked the abstract terms, he made do with clouds of ideas painted into the air, with comets whose traces he drew through the sunlit compartment with his finger.

Engelhardt asked his new travel friend whether he had heard of Swami Vivekananda. And when the latter said no, he unpacked from his valise several pamphlets, which he timidly laid out beside himself on the compartment seat. They were the writings of that selfsame swami, who had recently caused a furor in the New World by virtue of his unusual ideas and rhetorical talents. There, too, mimeographed and stitched together with a ribbon (the Franconian adhesive binding had disintegrated back in the southern Red Sea, near Aden, on account of intense exposure to heat), was his own treatise, the contents of which heralded the healing power of cocovorism, though unfortunately in German, such that Engelhardt might point to the volume as an object without, however, being able to articulate for his new friend the thoughts therein, which were considerably more skillfully phrased in written form.

And yet he did not wish to leave it untried; with some effort he paraphrased the fundamental notion in his text that man was the animal likeness of God and that the fruit of the coconut, in turn, which of all plants most resembled the human head (he was referring to the shape and hairs of the nut), was the vegetal likeness of God. It also grew, *nota bene*, closest to the heavens and the sun, high above atop the palm tree. Govindarajan nodded in assent and, as they passed through a small country station without stopping, was about to cite a relevant passage from the Bhagavata Purana (this was not the only sacred text he had had to memorize in his years of youth at the venerable University of Madras), when he resolved instead simply to continue nodding and let his interlocutor finish speaking in order, then, to note, with a certain gravitas he now deemed appropriate, that man, were he to subsist solely from the divine coconut, would not only be a cocovore, but also by definition a theophage. This he let resound for a moment in silence and then uttered the expression again into the stillness of midmorning, which was punctuated only by the clicking of the tracks: *God-eater. Devourer of God.*

Engelhardt was overwhelmed by that realization. Indeed, it cut him to the proverbial quick and began to take effect there as if it were a resounding, humming field of energy. Yes, indeed, the coconut—the delectable thought now revealed itself to him—was in truth the theosophical grail! The open shell with the meat and the sweet milk within was thus not just a symbol for, but in actual fact the body and blood of Christ. In his brief Catholic theology seminar in Nuremberg, he had heard it set forth in the same way, and now, on this tropical railroad journey, found it confirmed from quite a different perspective—the transubstantiating moment of the Eucharist could indeed be understood as physically becoming one with the divine. The host and Communion wine, however, couldn't be compared with the real sacrament of nature, his luscious, ingenious fruit: the coconut.

Govindarajan was quite evidently happy to have met a frugivore brother so serendipitously and then invited him—at that moment the train overcame one of the last hairpin turns, gasping and sputtering, and then straightened the course of its tracks toward the old Ceylonese royal city—to visit the Temple of the Tooth with him. They'd take a room in Kandy and, after a lavish fruit lunch, decamp together from there to the temple, which, Govindarajan claimed, lay but a few edifying steps from the city center on a small hill above Kandy Lake.

At the Queen's Hotel, they decided for reasons of cost to share a single room, which aroused a certain suspiciousness on the part of the receptionist that rapidly subsided, however, after Engelhardt placed a few banknotes on the counter, asserting that he very much wished to pay a gratuity in advance. One was accustomed to the eccentricities of the Anglo-Saxons, and if this German gentleman here wanted to sleep in the same room as a Tamil friend, then by all means. The question then arose whether one might expect the two gentlemen for lunch, whereupon both answered in English that a few papayas and pineapples would suffice entirely, but if a coconut were available, they would consider themselves fortunate to be served the coconut milk in a glass and the meat scooped onto a plate. The receptionist bowed, turned around, and disappeared off to the kitchen to place the two frugivores' order, rolling his eyes in annoyance.

Sated, rested despite the rail ride, and with the euphoric mood of a pair of pilgrims whose destination, long promised, now lay just within reach, the two strolled across the street and then leaned over a stone balustrade to find themselves reflected for a moment in the sacred lake, as lotus and frangipani blossoms floated on its surface. A group of bald-headed monks hurried by, chattering, each with a black rolled-up umbrella in his hand, their habits glowing saffron-yellow in the afternoon sun. A slender dandy in white flannel hurtled past on a penny-farthing, waving, honking the black squeeze bulb on his handlebars twice in quick succession. Govindarajan pointed with a cane (had he had one with him earlier?) toward the temple, and they then prepared to ascend the stairs leading up to the tabernacle.

The two pilgrims dabbed their moist foreheads with handkerchiefs, and, farther up, turned around to gaze down onto the artificial lake created by King Sri Vikrama Rajasinha at the beginning of the previous century. Govindarajan informed Engelhardt with a peculiar expression of satisfaction that fishing had been strictly forbidden from the start. The legend also went that the little temple island there in the middle of the lake had served the king of the Sinhalese as a clandestine site for bathing and sexual intercourse, and that a hidden tunnel under the lake led from the palace to this very island. Again Govindarajan raised his cane, and pointed in that direction with its end, which, Engelhardt suddenly discerned, consisted of beaten brass. Engelhardt noticed that the Tamil was smiling even more broadly than before, practically baring his teeth like a dog. His air and countenance, which had appeared to Engelhardt gentle and familiar while on the train journey, all of a sudden seemed overlaid with a stagy, shrill dissonance.

In the sultry interior of the shrine, a deep darkness of the most profound kind reigned supreme. A gong resounded with a muffled rattle, its echo rebounding unexpectedly from invisible walls that seemed to Engelhardt as if coated with slime. A single candle burned somewhere. He felt a mesmerizing sense of menace speed through his nerves; the blond hairs on his arms stood vertically on end, a rivulet of warm sweat pearling down behind his ear into his robe. Govindarajan had gone off elsewhere. The rapping of the metallic tip of his staff grew quieter and was eventually no longer perceptible, however much Engelhardt strained to hear it. The ghastly gong rang once more. And then the candle went out. Shuddering, he took a tentative step to the right and pivoted so as to face the point where he suspected the entrance to be—but upon entering the temple they had rounded several corners, barring which the light of day would likely have been visible from here. He whispered the name of his companion. Then he uttered it louder, finally shouting, *Go-vin-dara-jan!* into the inky dark.

No answer came. His friend had vanished. He had lured him here into the blackness and then absconded. But why? What if . . . ? And what-all in God's name had Engelhardt told him? He could no longer recall exactly, but he was sure he had told him about his luggage at the harbor in Colombo, had certainly confided in him as well that he was carrying a fairly large sum of money in bonds, which—he struck himself on the forehead with his palm in the darkness at the thought—he had of course left in his valise in their shared room at the Queen's Hotel. Engelhardt furiously loosened his hair tie and threw it on the floor. He had revealed everything to a complete stranger, to a passing acquaintance, in the belief that frugivorism created an invisible bond of solidarity between men. But perhaps the Tamil had simply fabricated everything? Maybe he hadn't been a vegetarian at all, but had merely said what he, Engelhardt, had wanted to hear.

Later, at the hotel—Engelhardt had been able to free himself, groping his way slowly out of the absurd captivity of the oppressively dank temple, which looked amicably innocuous and inviting as soon as he saw it again from without—he examined his travel bag, and in fact the sum of money he had sewn into one of its side pockets was missing. Otherwise, as far as he could tell, everything else was still there. Clutching his bag under his arm, he strode haltingly and almost on tiptoes down the stairs to the reception hall, informing the hotel employee in a whisper to please send the bill for his room to the consul of the German Reich in Colombo since he was unable to settle accounts. The hotelier cracked a crooked smile and replied that such an action was really unnecessary. No bill had accrued since there had been no overnight stay, the fruit breakfast was on the house, and furthermore he would advise a visit to the local police to report the Tamil, whom he had, incidentally, questioned ten or twenty minutes ago as to the

whereabouts of his German travel companion while he beat a
hasty retreat from the hotel, to which he had received no reply,
though he couldn't shake the feeling that the Tamil had perpe-
trated some act of malice, so guilty did he look.

The hotelier, who, by the way, was a splendid fellow, escorted
poor Engelhardt to the train station, sprang for his third-class
ticket down into the capital, and then, under minimal pro-
tests, steered the spindly young man, to whom a visit to the
local constabulary seemed the most disagreeable thing imaginable, into the last car of the slowly departing train. And there,
as he sits in the compartment (the afternoon, Prussian blue
and cloyingly fragrant, was now slipping into early evening),
his shoulder leaned against a fellow traveler, his back pressed
against the wooden seat, his eyes shut tight, his shaggy long
hair worn loose, his travel bag squeezed to his belly, the cinematograph suddenly begins to rattle: a cog loses its grip, the
moving pictures projected up front on the white canvas accel-
erate chaotically. Indeed, for a brief moment, they no longer
run forward as prescribed *ad aeternitatem* by the Creator, but
jolt, jerk, speed backward; Govindarajan and Engelhardt are
stepping into the air, feet poised—gay to watch—and hastening
backward down temple steps, crossing the street backward, too,
the projector beam flickering more and more severely, snapping
and crackling, and now, at an instant, everything loses shape
(since for a short while we are granted insight into the *bhavan-
tarabhava*, the moment of reincarnation), and then there appears, the right way up, of course, and in exact coloration and
frame rate, August Engelhardt, sitting in Herbertshöhe (New
Pomerania), in the reception room of the Hotel Fürst Bismarck,

there on a rattan sofa (of Australian manufacture) that might indeed be called snug. in conversation with Hotel Director Hellwig (Franz Emil), while balancing a cup of herbal tea on his knees, leaving the Ceylonese analepsis behind him. Hellwig is smoking.

III

This Hotel Director Hellwig, whose left ear, incidentally, was missing entirely, was known in Herbertshöhe not only as a broker for various and sundry, but also as the direct gateway to Mrs. Emma Forsayth, who had been recommended to Engelhardt by the incumbent Governor Hahl after he had made known by letter from Nuremberg his interest in the speedy acquisition of a coconut plantation. Do come, come to our merry colony, Hahl had written, but Engelhardt ought not expect *too* much civilization, though in its stead he would find quite a bit of adventure, largely diligent natives, and yes, absolutely, they had coconut palms in droves. Hahl's brisk epistolary style, a bit crude in spite of its eloquence, intimated that though he was from the Berlin area, within him dwelled a Bavarian intellectual, a hardheaded loner, which suited Engelhardt just fine. Hahl wrote further that he ought to join the German Club immediately after his arrival, if he pleased, and meet with said Mrs. Emma Forsayth, who owned various landholdings in the protectorate and was able to grant not only favorable credit for the purchase of a plantation to assiduous

planters from home (as long as she found them likable), but
could also procure good and reliable workers. She was quite the
celebrity, by the way. From New Pomerania to the Hawaiian islands, they called her simply Queen Emma. Engelhardt did not
give a second thought to conditions in the colony, where a
woman seemed to enjoy the same high status as the governor
himself, for he was, after having torn open the envelope with the
governor's seal, much too thrilled about the possibility of having
his reverie of cocovorism financed in advance. True, he had some
money set aside. Aunt Marthe had passed away two years ago
on the other side of the Swiss border and had remembered
him in her will; still, he couldn't scrape together more than
twenty thousand marks, minus those bonds lost to the Tamil
crook Govindarajan, of course.

Our friend had missed Governor Hahl by only a few days;
the hapless man had taken ill with blackwater fever and had
left the protectorate on the Italian passenger ship R.N. *Pasticcio*,
bound for Singapore, where he hoped to cure himself completely with quinine tonic while wrapped from head to toe in
cold wet sheets soaked in vinegar. Blackwater fever, as Hahl
was informed by his Indian physician during the passage, was
a complication of malaria, the carrier of which had recently
been ascertained as the common mosquito after centuries in
which people died without the slightest clue as to why. Hahl
was a strong man and quite accustomed to pain, and yet the
constantly recurring bouts of fever had depleted him and left
him hollow-cheeked and quietly despondent.

When he reached Singapore, however, he recalled suddenly, in a brief moment of inspired lucidity, not only those
letters from Nuremberg, but also the impressive young man

who had written them (Engelhardt had included a photograph that depicted him standing on a hill near Nuremberg, arms stretched aloft to the heavens, to the sun), and the arranged meeting in his Herbertshöhe residence, but just as swiftly, the next paroxysm overpowered him, his mind grew dark again, and Engelhardt's imago, which had seemed to him that of a radical new man by virtue of his letters (and this one photograph, which today, of course, has long since vanished), yielded once more to his illness's shiftless, dark brown realm of torment.

While still in Herbertshöhe, a few minutes before the mosquito—from whose erect proboscis the pathogens flowed into Hahl's bloodstream—had breathed its pitiful last under the slap of his hand (while the governor's crimson blood simultaneously pulsed through the insect's nervous system like sugary soma), he had had a dinner brought to him so he could work late while eating at the large mahogany table. Listlessly shoving the sweet potatoes and the chicken breast back and forth on the porcelain plate with his fork, he had skimmed correspondence and court decisions, had once more read the delightful letter from his friend Wilhelm Solf, the governor of Samoa, and in the process had drunk one and a half glasses of tropically tepid Riesling. It had been a calm, velvety night. He had placed a wax record on the gramophone turntable, setting the needle at his favorite spot, and while the first brassy bars of Wagner's *Ritt der Walküren* had tumbled through the salon, he had sneezed a few times, blown his nose into the napkin, then stretched out his limbs and loosened his tie, and at that precise moment, the insect had come buzzing up through the doorframe. Driven quite mad by the intense scent of lactic acid leaking from the Hahlian pores (the transpiration of which was eased and enhanced by the warm Riesling), the mosquito had extended its proboscis while still on the approach, landing, blind with greed, on the nape of the governor's cleanly shaven neck, and penetrating it with a cathartic, crescendo-like bite before suffering the redemptive Götterdämmerung of the palm of Hahl's hand. And this was how the blackwater fever had made its way into the governor.

And Engelhardt? Either he forgot to join the German Club or it no longer crossed his mind, since he felt absolutely no desire at all to socialize privately with those dim-witted, alcoholic planters who comprised the majority of the club members. While he was still at the Hotel Fürst Bismarck, where Director Hellwig had allowed him to lodge for the first week free of charge, gratis—in the expectation of certain perks in Herbertshöhe's hierarchy of prestige for his actions as an intermediary agent for Queen Emma vis-à-vis August Engelhardt (negotiations for purchasing a plantation were by no means an everyday occurrence in the protectorate)—Engelhardt had written around a dozen letters home and to his relatives in which he extolled the ravishing beauty of the colony in flowery, effusive words and urged his comrades-in-spirit to visit him here as quickly as possible.

He was, he wrote while letting his gaze wander from the hotel veranda over Herbertshöhe, in the middle of negotiations to purchase a plantation; just imagine the progressiveness: a woman conducted most business dealings here, and no one was irked even in the slightest by his long hair and his beard, so he had again proceeded to wear his hair down, though after heavy downpours it became comically wavy and tended to frizz outward in all directions due to the stifling humidity.

And, oh, that's right, he had had the pleasure of meeting a thoroughly likable young seaman at the hotel, a certain Christian Slütter, with whom he had engaged in a couple extended rounds of chess (in one, *solus rex* had been the result, in his favor), and had even undertaken several joint, exploratory constitutionals beyond the outskirts of the city. This man Slütter was on his way to acquiring his captain's license and was considering joining the Imperial Navy. He may not have been a vegetarian, but the discussions about the benefits and drawbacks of meat consumption, wherefore the flow of play had often been interrupted for hours on end, had taken place at such a high level and with such geniality that Engelhardt might not have had to leave Germany so quickly had similar conversations been possible with the uninitiated. But presumably one encountered these sorts of unprejudiced, open-minded characters like Slütter only overseas.

To the naturopath Adolf Just, to his friends at Jungborn and in the various nudist colonies of his homeland, he disclosed that the local weather conditions (the torrential downpours every afternoon he left unmentioned in these lines) were almost predestined to redound to the satisfaction and completeness of the sun worshipper. Indeed, the tropical solar radiation had had such a positive effect on the disposition and physical constitution that, from the second day of his stay, he had undertaken his walks through the capital of the protectorate barefoot, dressed only in a waistcloth around his loins. This was not entirely in accordance with the truth.

All the same, August Engelhardt must be defended against allegations that he was a liar, enticing future visitors to the South Seas (for there were more than a few who would heed his call) with statements of distorted and outright false fact. Engelhardt himself absolutely felt the compulsion to undress and present his skin to the soul-warming light; it was just that he found himself in the aforesaid negotiations to acquire a plantation, with monies he did not even possess, and so he was still sufficiently a pragmatist not to reveal immediately to all in Herbertshöhe his convictions regarding clothing and sustenance—after all, one didn't do business with naked, long-haired men.

At the Imperial Post Office, meanwhile, he became friendly with the stocky postmaster after they assured one another of their mutual enthusiasm for stamps of all kinds. The fellow led Engelhardt into the back room of the mail parlor and showed him a genuine little printery that the clerk ran there in his spare time: rubber cords, all sorts of seals, embossers, and printing matrices, labeled in a clean hand and organized into hundreds of small boxes attached to the wall; print samples of graphical elements and various letters lay on benches and tables next to one another. The protectorate had recently received its own stamps, which were now being furnished with the imperial seal *Deutsch Guinea* in the back parlor (on this very machine here). A light draft sprang up and swirled a few papers around that the official hurriedly gathered together again. Engelhardt was truly astonished. In his mind he already saw the official eagerly sketching drafts for his diverse advertising brochures. Back in the front office, he handed the official the letters for franking, slid a respectable gratuity across the counter, and the latter assured him he would see to it that his mailings would be

dispatched home safely on the next Imperial Post ship, Engelhardt could rely on him, may he come visit again soon.

Villa Gunantambu, Mrs. Forsayth's wooden palace, lay a few
minutes' walk from the forlorn placard marking the city limits
of Herbertshöhe. She herself sat on the veranda, a colorfully embroidered linen shawl draped around her slender, handsomely
shaped shoulders, and had air fanned at her by means of a complicated mechanical contraption. A naked little boy sat on the
lawn and blew soap bubbles that landed on Engelhardt's
shoulders, where, wearily and unspectacularly, like a metaphor
en miniature invoked by a second-class novelist, they breathed
their last brief, soapy breath.

And so he stepped onto the veranda, introduced himself,
and bowed. Mrs. Forsayth, though a half-caste, spoke excellent, one might even say overly perfect, German. Cold tea was
served, with pastries and tiny little cubes of mangosteen on
toothpicks, of which Engelhardt took a few mouthfuls so as
not to come across as impolite. Silence. Then, primarily to get
conversation going—for one look at the gaunt young man was
enough for her to classify him as a shy fellow who had turned
his back on life somewhat—Mrs. Forsayth pointed out the ca-
suarina trees growing adjacent to her wooden palace, thickly
festooned with fruit bats that dangled like cocoons from the
leafless boughs and occasionally flailed about with their pata-
gia, screeching. During high heat, she declared, fixing her gaze
sternly on Engelhardt, the animals urinated over their own
wings, and the evaporative cold produced by flapping then provided the desired cooling effect. Engelhardt cleared his throat
and smiled awkwardly, an indefinable tone of discord rattling
forth from his gullet.

Mrs. Forsayth intimidated him. She was, after all, despite being long past fifty and corpulent, a highly attractive woman who knew how to complement her flattering facial expressions most arrestingly with scant but resolute movements. It may well be that Engelhardt allowed himself to be overawed (and indeed, the businesswoman Emma Forsayth would not have been sitting there were she not thrice as shrewd as her male colleagues), for he hemmed and hawed a bit, haltingly mentioned the correspondence with Governor Hahl, and then outlined his plan to harvest the fruits of the coconut palm and trade in the by-products, which is to say, not just in copra; he also wanted to produce oils and creams and send them off, attractively labeled, back into the Reich. He even envisioned inventing a shampoo; he described the fragrant coconut essence in the hair of ladies in fine Berlin societies, in his reasoning furtively bearing in mind that, in the end, Mrs. Forsayth was perhaps just a woman who occasionally longed to return to places not lacking in opera houses, hackneys, and luxuriously perfumed sitz baths with constant hot water. In addition and above all, he added, he had come to German New Guinea to establish a kind of commune that would pay homage to the coconut.

Queen Emma ignored Engelhardt's last sentence, which in any case was declaimed rather more inaudibly than his plans for the economic exploitation of *Cocos nucifera*. And the flattering words about coconut shampoo did not impress her in the least. So he wished to buy a plantation? She had exactly the thing for him. A little island! Yet wouldn't Engelhardt perhaps first want to explore the interior and think about whether he might like a larger-scale plantation there, albeit in a hard-to-reach location? Depending on the weather, a four- or five-day journey away, that is, around sixty miles from Herberts-höhe as the crow flies, there was a coconut planting of some twenty-five hundred acres whose owner—indeed, one must needs state it without hesitation—had gone mad and doused himself, his family, and three black employees with pitch and set them alight. That plantation could be had, considering its size, for nearly nothing, since the planter's will, written in a state of complete mental barbarism, could not be validated (*Kill them all* could be read in it) and the estate thus passed to the German Reich, and in particular to the firm Forsayth & Company, the director of which was sitting here before him.

The island Kabakon, she continued, had only one hundred eighty-five acres of coconut palms, although it had the ad-vantage of being located but a few nautical miles away from Herbertshöhe somewhat to the north in the Neu-Lauenburg archipelago. An island would be both manageably sized and easy to cultivate. One needed only harvest and process the coconuts. One might then transport the yield by boat and of-fer it for sale in Herbertshöhe, avoiding the arduous and dan-gerous path through the jungle that the haul would have to travel from the large inland plantation. Anyway, what an is-land, she rhapsodized: every year, the inhabitants of Kabakon sent a canoe out to sea laden with cowries and adorned with green leaves to compensate the fish for their relatives caught the previous year. And there was a charming tradition at wed-dings: a coconut was broken open over the heads of the couple and the coconut milk spilled out over them. The isle cost forty thousand marks, as did the gigantic plantation in the interior. Engelhardt exhaled audibly.

Now, she could give him these two quotes, but he ought

to have a look at both, please, and then decide. She likely knew
that she had not only made the decision easy for him, but
forced it with a steady hand—the plantation of the fellow gone
mad was cheaper many times over but tainted for him with
such bad kismet on account of her description of its circumstances that Engelhardt would choose the island Kabakon. In
the end, she was a businesswoman, and if this young eccentric—
for she had certainly heard that Engelhardt wanted to found
an order of coconut-eaters, and Governor Hahl had of course
reported on him already, too—wanted to leave his money
with her, then so be it. Besides, well, she liked him, liked how
he sat there, bearded, ascetic, with his impossible hair and
those aqua-colored eyes, skinny as a sparrow.

She couldn't help thinking of a visit to Italy many years
ago; it was as if she had already seen Engelhardt there before,
but where? Yes! Of course! That was it! In the work of the
Florentine master Fra Angelico, in his depictions of the savior
Jesus Christ as martyr. Engelhardt was the spitting image of the
Redeemer in those portraits. She smiled blithely and for a few
seconds sank away into that golden, long-bygone afternoon after the visit to the church of San Marco, into that discreet tryst
at the little pensione not far from the Arno.

As a nearly unbelievable coincidence would have it, Engelhardt had in fact also been in Florence at that very same time.
After the obligatory visit to the Santa Croce, he had wanted to
climb up to San Miniato al Monte, but since the dismal poverty
of the Italians beyond the city gate of Porta Romana rattled
him—he saw heavyset, leather-aproned butchers with their
cleavers, hacking into pieces of meat riddled with yellow fat;
people were throwing excrement out of their windows into

the Via Romana at night, as if still in the depths of the Dark
Ages—had sought a shortcut through the Boboli Gardens
and sat there on a stone bench to rest, slipped off his sandals,
and then languorously stretched out his feet. Somewhere unseen, an amateur had been practicing the trombone. On the
hills beyond the city, cypresses shot abruptly into the hyper-
blue sky like black flames.

Sitting across the way on this side of the gravel path had
been a gaunt, ascetic-seeming man wearing a small pair of steel
spectacles, whose visage the Florentine Easter sun had already
burnt a deep nut-brown hue; he had been reading from a book
and was, please note, not an Italian, but likely a Swede or a
Norwegian. Each had seen the other; the novelist—for that was
what he probably was, and not a Scandinavian, but a Swabian—
had sized the young bearded man up with interest, before de-
ciding not to address him, although the gentleman who had
been so appraised seemed to hope he would. And then both
had gone their separate ways, Engelhardt up to San Miniato al
Monte and the Swabian writer off to a simple tavern in the San
Niccolò district, where, ensconced in a cool corner, he had
ordered a piece of cured ham and a quarter liter of blood-red
Valpolicella, continued work on a manuscript with the somewhat plain title *Gertrud*, and quickly forgotten the young man.

Engelhardt finished his tea, glancing at the thin, precious
Chinese porcelain of the cup in his hand and the rich woman
smiling obligingly there on the canapé before him, and heard
the word *Kabakon* whispered ever so softly in his mind. He
placed the cup back onto the tray carefully and said he would
take the island, sight unseen; he would pay sixteen thousand
marks in cash, borrowing the rest, if she wouldn't mind, against

his own production. Queen Emma did not deliberate for long; here a wispy little Jesus was coming to her wanting to pay sixteen thousand marks for a worthless islet without haggling and, on top of that, pledged to sign over his entire yield to her for two years—a quick, rough approximation—and all this for a little piece of land she had inveigled from a Tolai chief for two old rifles, a crate of axes, two sails, and thirty pigs. She offered her hand rather entrancingly, without getting up; Engelhardt took it, and they shook in agreement.

A contract was drawn up, copies were sent back and forth between Villa Gunantambu and the Hotel Fürst Bismarck, secretly perused by Hotel Director Hellwig (who quite inappropriately stuck his red-veined nose and his single ear into everything), signed by Engelhardt, and adorned with an inky blue thumbprint. Long walks were taken, several jars of iodine, three mosquito nets, and two steel axes were purchased, and arrangements were made to send his crates of books after him; otherwise, Engelhardt took nothing over from this prosaic world into his own.

The sun shone, oh, how it shone. The passage over to Mioko with the steam launch proceeded quickly and without incident. Upon arrival there, a taciturn German-Russian agent named Botkin gestured with his thumb toward a sailing canoe hoisted up onto the beach and at the ready, and revealed to Engelhardt that it was his, take it, he owned three of them, even. Two natives came along; no one said a word. Engelhardt stripped off his sandals and knee socks, taking a seat on the rear bench, and in a single forward movement they cruised to Kabakon under a full sail that billowed magnificently in the east wind. Flying fish accompanied the canoe, leaping parabolas of silver. He tasted the salty ocean air, wiggled his naked big toes back and forth, and swore to himself, smiling, not to put his sandals back on anytime soon. After a good half hour, the green outlines of his isle appeared on the horizon. One of the men pointed over toward it with the stump of his arm and looked back over his shoulder with a smile, his perfect white teeth showing, two tightly closed rows of ivory.

To own one's own island on which the coconut grew and flourished in the wild! It had not yet fully penetrated Engelhardt's consciousness, but now as the little boat glided from the open ocean into the calmer, transparent waters of a small bay, the brightly conjured shore of which was lined with majestically soaring palms, his heart began fluttering up and down like an excited sparrow. My goodness, he thought, this was now really his! All this!

He leapt from canoe into water, waded the last few yards to the shore, and fell to his knees in the sand, so overcome was he; and for the black men in the boat and the few natives who had found their way to the beach with a certain phlegmatic curiosity (one of them even wore a bone fragment in his lower lip, as though he were parodying himself and his race), it looked as if a pious man of God were praying there before them; it might remind us civilized peoples of a depiction of the landing of the conquistador Hernán Cortés on the virginal shore of San Juan de Ulúa, perhaps painted by turns—if this were even possible—by El Greco and Gauguin, each of whom, with an expressive, jagged stroke of the brush, once more conferred upon the kneeling conqueror Engelhardt the ascetic features of Jesus Christ.

Thus, the seizure of the island Kabakon by our friend looked quite different depending on the viewpoint from which one observed the scenario and who one actually was. This splitting of reality into various components was, however, one of the chief characteristics of the age in which Engelhardt's story takes place. To wit: modernity had dawned; poets suddenly wrote fragmented lines; grating and atonal music, which to unschooled ears merely sounded horrible, was premiered before audiences who shook their baffled heads, was pressed into records and reproduced, not to mention the invention of the cinematograph, which was able to render our reality exactly as tangible and temporally congruent as it occurred; it was as if it were possible to cut a slice of the present and preserve it in perpetuity between the perforations of a strip of celluloid.

All this, however, did not move Engelhardt; he was on his way toward withdrawing not only from modernity dawning the world over, but altogether from what we non-Gnostics denote as progress, as, well, civilization. Engelhardt took a decisive step forward onto the shore; in reality, it was a step back into a barbarism most exquisite.

The first hut was erected according to the manner of the natives. Makeli appeared now, too, for the first time, a perhaps thirteen-year-old boy who came trudging through the mangroves sometime in the afternoon, timidly but obstinately, walked onto Engelhardt's white-sand stage, and was never seen to budge from his side again. Six men came and showed him how to intertwine palm leaves with one another to weave a roof and walls. They gave him fruits, and he quenched his thirst; they gave him a lap-lap, he stripped naked, they cloaked his belly with it, and tied off the ends below his navel; the sun stabbed down from the sky with merciless vehemence; soon his shoulders were burnt red.

Makeli chose the place where the hut was to stand; a clearing was cut from the shore into the bush, some corner posts were rammed into the exposed marshy soil, which had first been dried for a few hours in the sun by removing the overstory, and the mats of palm fronds that had been created in the meantime were now woven together. Engelhardt, whose shyness had made him seem so unfit for life in our world, but which among these savages seemed whisked away by a fresh, jocose breeze, eagerly took part in the collective wattling. Now and again, he ran down to the shore and scooped cooling ocean water onto his burning shoulders with both hands. Small children would run with him then, throwing themselves naked and screeching and grinning before him into the surges, and Engelhardt laughed with them.

The first night, he lay on the sand floor he himself had shoveled into the hut on top of the marshy, still slightly wet clay ground and decided after some unpleasant tossing and turning that henceforth he would sleep elevated on a bedstead or a wicker cot. The sand may have been soft, but it trickled into his ear if he made himself comfortable on his side in the fetal position. On the other hand, if he lay on his back, he found the back of his head and the long hair underneath scratched by the sand in the most aggravating manner (the heat and humidity had crumbled his hair band into disintegrating bits). And he had scarcely calmed himself, saying nothing more could be done tonight to make sleep more bearable, and tomorrow morning we'll see how a bed can be built—he was drifting off to sleep, smiling almost contentedly about his own Buddhist-seeming indifference to discomfort—when he became aware of hundreds of mosquitoes that had chosen to punish his skin with extremely painful bites. For a long while he slapped at them in the dark helplessly and pitifully and then set fire to a coir mat. Its heavy emission of smoke successfully drove the mosquitoes from his hut but made him cough with such unbridled force, while at the same time bringing stifling tears to his burning eyes, that he buried his face in a sand pit and, enraged, awaited the hour at which first sunlight would finally break through the holes in the fringy rattan walls.

The following late afternoon he recalled the mosquito nets brought along from Herbertshöhe, unpacked one from its cardboard container, unfolded it, and hung it with great circumspection from the walls and ceiling of his rattan hut. A small rip that resulted from the process he mended with two or three skillful sutures. Then he tentatively lay down beneath it, smiling at his unyieldingness; someone else might have considered leaving. He harbored the greatest fear of the fever and ardently hoped he had not been bitten last night by an infected insect; on the other hand, that was simply the price one had to pay here. In Germany, there were few diseases whose course brought about such horrific repercussions: instead, one had to suffer an infestation of the mind an inner, incurable rottenness, the corrosive power of which was capable of eating through the soul like a cancerous ulcer.

Now, one cannot avoid saying that the inhabitants of Kabakon knew nothing whatsoever of the fact that the little island on which they had lived for as long as anyone could remember suddenly no longer belonged to them but to the

young *witeman* whom they had amicably taken in at the behest of the agent Botkin, for whom they built a hut, and to
whom they had brought fruit. And at the outset it was by
no means Engelhardt's intention to conduct himself like an
especially stern island king; but, returning to his hut one afternoon from an exploratory walk around the two wooded
hills, he chanced upon the following scene.

There, in a glade, a boy had ensnared a pitch-black piglet,
which he was dragging around by its tail. A young man joined
him, raising a heavy wooden club, and sending it hurtling down
with a crack onto the animal's head; the pig immediately collapsed dead with an abject squeal. Then three or four black
women attacked it, opening the pig's belly with a sharp shard,
throwing the entrails to the side, and expertly scraping out the
innards.

Engelhardt, who imagined himself on the one hand to be
lord over the isle and thus over the doings of its inhabitants as
well, but who on the other hand intended to countenance the
natives' customs, gallantly intervened, snatching the shiv from
the woman carrying the cutting implement, and sending it flying into the bush. In so doing, he slipped on a piece of intestine
and fell belly-first into the sandy puddle of blood. That, as it
happened, was his salvation, because instead of letting the
same fate as the pig befall the lanky *witeman* (the fellow with
the club had already taken a step forward), everyone in the
glade began to laugh their heads off at Engelhardt's capriole.
The latter stood up, besmirched with blood from head to toe,
rubbing the dark red sand from his eyes, and the native with
the club lowered his weapon, took Engelhardt's hand in his
with a laugh, slapped the German on the back companion-

ably, and henceforth it was clear that the slaughtering of animals would take place on the other side of the little island. Engelhardt was, the natives told one another, a greater *witeman* than they thought; he had shown courage in intervening, even if they didn't quite understand why he didn't want them to kill and gut pigs. Engelhardt, they agreed among themselves, possessed the magic *mana*, and thus he was allowed to remain on Kabakon as long as he saw fit.

The next morning, nearly forty men stood before Engelhardt's hut and indicated in a hodgepodge of Kuanua, German Creole, and pidgin that they intended to work for the German man. They wished to be in his employ and collect the coconuts from the trees and process them. Engelhardt stood atop a piece of driftwood and stated in a pantomimic speech that he was no missionary, heavens, no, that he looked much forward to their industriousness, that he would pay them punctually, that the coconut and the palm tree were sacred, and that he intended to subsist from it alone. For that reason he would suffer no meat in his vicinity and would ask of his workers (here he paused for a moment—was he perhaps going too far?), at least while they were working on his plantation, not to eat pork or chicken. The men nodded sagely, especially as the consumption of these animals was reserved for the yearly feasts and as they only chewed on yams during the day anyway, if need be drinking from a few coconuts like Engelhardt himself. Were eggs perhaps allowed? one of the men wanted to know. Another inquired about smoking. And might they be permitted to drink liquor? Engelhardt replied readily, and it seemed to him as if his new workers thought the whole matter an amusing game. Jumping down from the tree trunk, he said that was enough queries for now, and his islanders immediately appeared to accept the authority with which he had impressed upon them the Kabakonian policies that would govern them henceforth.

With one stroke, Engelhardt seemed to have conquered his fear, the fear of uncertainty, his fear of not having enough money or sustenance, of what his fellow man thought of him, the fear that he would seem ridiculous, his fear of loneliness, his fear of not being loved or of doing the wrong thing—all this had fallen away from him as the clothing he no longer wore or was capable of wearing, since the trousers and shirts (even the lap-lap he now doffed on his walks along the beach, hesitatingly at first, then with ever greater naturalness) seemed to him symbols of an outmoded outside world long since grown weary. He lived in immaculate, splendid isolation. No one took even the slightest notice of his nakedness. Since the incident with the piglet, they respected him, offered him a friendly good morning when they encountered him in the forest, and treated him like one of their own. He in fact did bear the magical *mana* within his tender breast.

Together with young Makeli, he roamed naked across the island, only a sack over his shoulder, and the indigenous boy showed Engelhardt the locations that were *tabu* for him: mostly ancestral burial grounds or certain glades. They shook the bristly palm trunks until enough fruits had fallen down. One needed only bend over to harvest these treasures! Makeli showed him how to lever one's way up the trunk into the treetop by means of a coir rope slung around one's waist, a knife in one's adept hands, to get to all the delectable nuts that hadn't been felled by jiggling alone.

After nightfall, he sat down with Makeli on the sandy floor of his hut and read to the boy from a book by the sparse light of a coconut-oil lamp, and although the latter understood almost nothing at first, he still harkened attentively to the foreign sound of the words that took shape, through Engelhardt's lips as he mouthed them, from the gently turned pages of the book; it was a German translation of Dickens's *Great Expectations*, and gradually the young islander seemed to grow accustomed to the foreign language and long for those hours, every evening, of being read to.

Makeli had listened to a preacher reading from a German Bible many times before, to be sure, but this was something quite different, for Engelhardt's utterances were more mellifluous, friendlier, and sweeter, and he picked up this or that word; more than anything else he seemed to like the descriptions of the house belonging to the crotchety spinster Miss Havisham, who, in her cobwebbed bedroom, sat like a primordial, misanthropic spider, receiving visitors with a sullen look. The boy tried to understand; after a few weeks of listening, through his repetition of some words in German Creole and his own translation of others into pidgin, terse German sentences began to form on his tongue.

Yet this was play and amusement—for their part, the natives worked with enormous efficiency; the nuts were collected with large trap baskets, cut into slices, and dried in the sun on timbered racks, protected by a rain shelter made of palm fronds, then, in a prehistoric-seeming mill consisting of little more than roughly hewn boulders, squeezed into oil, which was finally funneled into wooden barrels and taken to Herbertshöhe by Engelhardt's fleet of sailing canoes. There it was refined through filtering and heat and poured into bottles that Engel-hardt had borrowed from the ubiquitous Forsayth & Company. Now and again, a freighter anchored off the white breakers at the arch of the reef and took aboard the unprocessed copra. Engelhardt paid his employees punctually, as promised. Ini-tially, they demanded that he disburse their wages in cowrie shells or tobacco; later, when they learned what all could be had in Herbertshöhe, it had to be in marks. So as not to have to hide German currency on his isle, he issued them simple prom-issory notes that he signed and urged them to redeem in the capital. And every two months he traveled over himself in his lap-lap and, amid the disapproving looks of the planters dressed in white and their wives, paid his employees' debts.

IV

When was it that our friend first surfaced in the ocean of consciousness? All too little is known about him; within the narrative current, people and events flash by like fleet fish sparkling brightly underwater and Engelhardt flanks them as if he were one of those little creatures called *Labrichthyini* that clean the skin of other, larger predatory fish by freeing them from parasites and debris.

We see him, again on a train, for instance, but now traveling from—just a moment—Nuremberg to Munich; he's back there, standing third class, his slender hand, rather sinewy already for his young age, resting on a walking stick.

The old century draws to an unbelievably rapid close (the new century may also have begun already); it's almost autumn, Engelhardt is wearing, as he does everywhere in Germany when he isn't naked, a long pale cotton tunic and woven footwear with a Roman aspect, though not fashioned from animal leather. His hair, worn down on both sides of his face, reaches to his sternum; over his arm he's carrying a wicker basket with apples and pamphlets in it. Children riding along in the train are afraid of him, hide on the platform between cars of the second and third class, watching him; they laugh at him. One of the braver ones chucks a piece of sausage at him but misses. Mumbling absentmindedly, Engelhardt reads in a timetable the names of the provincial towns, familiar to him still from childhood, and then gazes again straight out onto the Bavarian landscape racing past; today is some sort of holiday, the country stations they speed through are all merrily flagged with black, white, and red pennants, the less martial pale blue of his homeland flying in between. Engelhardt is not someone interested in politics; the great upheavals carpeting the German Reich in recent months leave him completely cold. He has been keeping himself too far removed from society and its capricious vagaries and political fads. It is not he who is alien to the world, but the world that has become a stranger to him.

Having arrived in midmorning Munich, he visits his comrade Gustaf Nagel in Schwabing; long-haired, they stroll across the late-summer Odeonsplatz shrouded in linen amid the clamorous ridicule of the city folk. A besabered gendarme briefly considers whether he ought to arrest them, but then quickly decides against it, not wanting to let his glass of after-work beer go flat on account of additional paperwork.

The Feldherrnhalle, that Florentine parody off yonder, scarcely dignified by a glance, stands admonishingly, indeed almost slyly, in Munich's spectral summer light. In just a few short years, the time for it to play a leading part in the great Theater of Darkness will finally come. Flags with the Hindu sun cross will festoon it impressively and then, climbing the three or four steps to the stage, a squat vegetarian, an absurd black toothbrush mustache under his nose, will . . . oh, let's just wait for it to commence somberly (in Aeolian minor), that Great German Death Symphony. It might be comical to watch, were unimaginable cruelty not to ensue: bones, excreta, smoke.

Unaware of all this, Nagel and Engelhardt sun their legs and thighs in the English Garden, tunics hiked up, encircled for a while by the buzzing of sleepy bees; afterward, they travel out together to Murnau, south of Munich's gates, and there seek out—it's getting to be evening—a farmer friend of theirs who has gotten it into his square head to carry out his farm work naked the whole sweet summer long. Mahogany-brown, he stands before them at the fence, hatless, muscles bulging, extending his manly paw to greet the two slight, learned youths. Although it's already September, they take off their tunics, take a seat at the simple wooden table in front of the farmstead; the farmer's good wife brings her husband bread, fat, and ham, and apples and grapes for the two visitors, her naked breasts swaying like heavy gourds over the table as she sets it. A shy, slender milkmaid, likewise nude, joins them at the farmer's invitation. Our friend lays down a few pamphlets; they take pleasure in the solidarity of sun worshippers, eating of the fruit. An oriole sings happily in the tree above them.

Presently, Engelhardt speaks of the coconut, which of course neither the peasant, nor his wife, nor the farm girl has ever tasted or seen. He tells of the idea of encircling the globe with coconut colonies, rising from his seat (his almost pathological shyness vanishes when he champions his cause as an orator before sympathetic ears), speaking of the sacred duty of one day paying homage to the sun, naked, in the Temple of Palms. Only here—and he gestures around himself with outstretched arms—it will not work, unfortunately: too long the inhospitable winter, too narrow the minds of the Philistines, too loud the machines of the factories. Engelhardt climbs from the bench onto the table and down again, exclaiming his credo that only those lands in eternal sunlight will survive and, in them, only those people who allow the salutary and beneficent rays of the daystar to caress skin and head, unfettered by clothing. These brothers and sisters here have made a promising start, he says, but they really must now sell their farm and follow him, leaving Bavaria as Moses left Egypt of old and booking passage on a ship to the equator.

Is it to be Mexico or perhaps even Africa? Nagel wants to know while the peasant couple prepare more sandwiches, listening attentively. Engelhardt is, Nagel notes, obsessed with his ideas; they are like a little demon that has seized hold of him, tearing with a row of pointy teeth. He wonders for a moment if Engelhardt is still quite right in the head. Mexico—no, no, it has to be the South Seas, only there can and will it begin. High into the white and blue sky, he jabs his index finger; down onto the wooden table hammers Engelhardt's slender little fist. Although the dazzling sfumato of his mindscape is served up with great demagogic skill, little, it would seem, stays with the honest peasant couple; the serpentine paths of Engelhardtian fancy wend too wildly.

Later at night, in the haystacks where it smells of the dust of the long summer, Nagel and Engelhardt lie next to one another, discussing at a whisper, forging plans and discarding them again, and Nagel realizes just how much he appreciates his friend and how much more radically than his own Engelhardt's thoughts push out into the world. A cat moans above in the darkness of the timbers. Nagel seriously considers following his friend to the colonies: factors in favor would include that the ridicule poured out over him daily, endured for endless years, threatens to crush his soul slowly; that he has begun to doubt the integrity of his actions; and that Engelhardt, along with his obsessiveness, seems to him a leader who by virtue of his brilliance is capable of guiding him, Nagel, out of the dull wasteland that is Germany and into a bright, moral, pure pasture, not just metaphorically, but *in realitas*. On the other hand, however—and Nagel's anima already beholds the portals of the land of Nod—he is also too lazy, plain and simple, to betake himself around the globe to create a new Germany at the back of beyond. No, he muses just before the realm of shades welcomes him, he will henceforth write his name in lowercase, eschewing capitalization entirely, will always write everything small, like this: gustaf nagel. That will be his revolution. And then sleep comes.

August Engelhardt is now seen again, far to the north, traveling toward Berlin; he has parted ways with Gustaf Nagel at the Munich central station, each having clasped the other's forearms in heartfelt fellowship. Nagel is still advising him to make the journey to Prussia *per pedes* for ideological reasons, but Engelhardt replies that he must save time since he still has so much planned in the South Seas, and should his friend change his mind again, he will always and most sincerely be welcome.

Engelhardt, who is traversing the empire in express trains, likewise changes his mind just outside of Berlin, bypasses that gigantic, monstrous anthill, and boards a train to Danzig, sleeping on wooden benches, patiently awaiting connections, changing trains again, over and over, arrives in Königsberg and Tilsit, and travels northwest again, toward Prussian Lithuania.

There, spat out by the train in East Prussia's Memel, shouldering his bindle, he walks through the groves of birch trees blown through by the north wind, quitting the dull brick town, buys currants and mushrooms from a Russian babushka who crosses herself, taking him in his penitential robe for a Molokan apostate of Orthodoxy, sights the spare, milky-white wooden church marking the edge of the lagoon over there, marches in a southerly direction toward that spit of land, wondering as he rambles whether perhaps the German soul might come from this place, here, from this infinitely melancholy, sixty-mile-long, sunlit strand of dunes where he undresses, at first somewhat timidly, then with increasing confidence, placing his robe and his sandals in a depression in the sand (it is now early evening), and, concealing his nakedness from a couple of summering vacationers dressed in fine white cloth who are sauntering at some distance (he the editor of *Simplicissimus*, slight ironic twist to the mouth under the groomed mustache, gesticulating; she a freethinking daughter of a mathematician, nodding to him in agreement, in a dress of her own design), stares out onto the Baltic Sea long after the couple disappear and darkness descends, letting the plan to travel forever and for all time to the German overseas territories in the Pacific Ocean, never to return, ripen slowly in his mind, like a small child who has proceeded to build an immense castle out of colorful little wooden blocks. A gentle and somber Lithuanian melody drifts across the shoal, unapproachable like the stars flashing wanly in the firmament and yet immeasurably familiar, sweet, and homey: *Wuchsen einst fünf junge Mädchen schlank und schön am Memelstrand. Sing, sing was geschah? Keines den Brautkranz wand. Keines den Brautkranz wand.*

In the morning, three policemen with sabers come and cement Engelhardt's decision. In Memel the previous evening, the editor, who had indeed seen the nudist on the beach, filed a complaint with the police. There is a long-haired vagabond lying about the sandbars, stark-naked, scarcely two miles south down the strip of dunes. The editor deftly maneuvered his betrothed around the delinquent at some distance, distracting her at the crucial moment by showing her a flock of migratory birds or some such thing on the horizon, and yes, it is indeed a thing of outrage; one ought to arrest him; no, he did not seem drunk.

Engelhardt awakens, peeps out of the wind-sheltered hollow he had dug for himself that night, and sees three pairs of boots standing before him, uniform trousers tucked into them; the slight chill of the summer night is still in him, a tattered blanket is tossed down and the order given, in the gruffest commanding tone, tinged with Lithuanian, to follow them to Memel; the vagabond is being placed under arrest, offending public decency being the very least they intended to charge him with.

One of the gendarmes (he isn't the brightest) places his booted foot in front of Engelhardt—who has barely had time to pull himself together, wrap himself in the scratchy army blanket, and stand up—causing him to stumble and fall face-first into the sand again. Wicked laughter. Actually, they are all three not the brightest sort. As he is lying before them on the ground, an animalistic and cruel desire to humiliate infects them (for they are officious German subjects), and they begin kicking him and working him over with their fists; the ringleader strikes him on the back with the pommel of his saber since Engelhardt has curled up into a ball to escape the blows. He seeks refuge in white-frothy, buzzing unconsciousness.

After they've dunked him in the cleansing sea—suddenly and rather dimly aware that what they are doing is quite wrong and that Engelhardt isn't moving anymore—they comb his disheveled hair, wipe the still-flowing blood from his mouth and nostrils, dress him in the smock and sandals they've found not far from the sandy hollow, and take him (he's half carried, half walking on his own) to the police station in Memel, where, accused of vagrancy and immorality, he spends what might be deemed a quite agonizing night on a hard wooden bench, surveying for hours the deepest corners of the detention cell's ceiling with one eye (the other eye is swollen shut).

The editor and his bride left for Munich by daybreak, the incident nearly forgotten already; they are sitting across from one another in the dining car of the adjoining wagon-lit; railroad-induced stains from a bottle of Trollinger, ordered in a moment of airy mischief, have splotched the tablecloth with purple hue. The conversation isn't quite flowing, be it from fatigue or perhaps from an already anticipated sense of the boredom that will set in after years of marriage. With a mild lack of enthusiasm, the editor's gaze tracks left, out through the darkening pane of train glass, which grows more and more mirrorlike by the minute, onto the fading East Prussian plain, and he suddenly becomes aware of the almost boyishly slender shoulders of the naked young man lying on the beach yesterday, and he recognizes at this moment the actual reason he lodged a complaint, and that his whole future life will be, must be, covered over in painful self-deception, the immensity of which will discolor everything until his dying day—the still-unborn children, the work (for several novels are ripening within him), the still-amused relationship to the ideal of his own bourgeois sensibility, and the now-nascent revulsion at those hands there, folded in elegant calm on the dining car table, of his patiently smiling fiancée, who in turn will persist in decades of ignorance, though her propensity to behave and dress with a certain unwomanliness might have given the young girl, perhaps even now at the outset of their relationship, an indication vis-à-vis the actual proclivities of her betrothed.

On the afternoon of the following day, August Engelhardt is released. A delegation of activists did not balk at the long journey from Danzig, among them a solicitor licensed by the Imperial Court of Justice, who, obtaining entry to the detention cell, casts but one glance at Engelhardt and his wounds and immediately roars into the ears of the Memel constables a philippic recited in a furious stentorian voice: they should count themselves fortunate if they still hold a job this evening and are not in fetters, dishonored, and forever stripped of their uniforms, on their way to the dungeons of a special police purgatory (wherever this might be).

The completely overwhelmed gendarmes flit nervously through the office, variously colored papers and carbon copies waft about, the constable who first tripped Engelhardt on the beach even salutes the solicitor most humbly as if he were His Majesty the Kaiser himself. They hurry to release Engelhardt immediately, and the activists almost carry him on their hands out of the Memel police station, shouting, *Vivat!*, *Freedom!*, and *Down with violence!*

A crowd of townsfolk gathers in the market square—there are perhaps fifty or sixty of them, though their number seems somewhat higher than it is in reality—while the report of the hermit's abuse is passed from ear to ear, altered slightly with each further telling, so that ultimately the news goes around that a Catholic priest passing through from Avignon was tortured at the mercy of the local police and that the mayor, who has since come running, was in fact already in Tilsit requesting relief and replacement for the now-intolerable Memel constabulary.

Engelhardt is maneuvered into a first-class compartment of the Prussian State Railways. There they bed him on cooling sheets, two down pillows are thrust under his head, and after he refuses with a gesture of mild revulsion the fresh cow's milk that the doctor on board considerately hands him, he is given a half pint of unfiltered apple juice to drink, while a likable and, in her own way, even quite charming Frisian female activist (in a starched gown bulging over her tremendous bosom) pats the back of his slackened hand. She smells, it seems to Engelhardt, of mild cheese rind, but perhaps it's just the spurned, jittery glass of milk over in the corner of the compartment, in the convex opacity of which nothing at all is reflected. I do not believe he has ever truly loved anyone.

Berlin is groaning under a high pressure system that has lasted now for weeks on end and, beginning down in the Ottoman Empire, pushing up through Central Europe, has blanketed the city so stiflingly that a populace mutinying against the heat hijacks ice-cream carts, wet handkerchiefs are worn on heads, and fire engines have been commandeered and sent to the Zoological Garden to hose down the animals howling from heat and thirst. When Engelhardt's train from Danzig arrives at Schlesischer Bahnhof, though, it is as if a needle were inserted in a balloon: within minutes, the flaying heat bursts, towering clouds gather, piling themselves over the city, and instantly it pours and dumps down in unimaginable, outrageous floods. Streams of water tumble down in cascades, the rain in places so impenetrable that it links building fronts on adjacent street corners like a solid aquatic wall; muslin umbrellas are of precious little use here. People drape themselves in black-rubberized rain capes (all the caoutchouc required for the varnish is imported from the brutish slave plantations of the Belgian Congo) and proceed, like crows strutting aslant, against the pelting rain now blowing sideways, now pouring down from above, now pushing from behind.

The city is one large construction zone; holes as deep as a man hinder orderly passage, and these are now filling with brackish water, to boot. Siberian traders sell their soggy bric-a-brac at Alexanderplatz, where there's also extremely inexpensive bratwurst to be had, consisting mainly of meat scraps and moldy flour, that disintegrates immediately in the rain. The tram, creaking and throwing sparks, shoves past decent citizens, who jump onto the footstep to avoid the most severe showers of all; everywhere, dripping iron cranes strain heavenward. This, then, is Berlin, a mediocre, slovenly, provincial town, carelessly erected in the sands of Brandenburg, masquerading as an imperial capital.

After learning that Silvio Gesell, whom he wanted to consult here in Berlin on founding a moneyless vegetarian community, has since emigrated to Argentina, Engelhardt escapes the small throng of his liberators in the bustle of Schlesischer Bahnhof, leaps into a horse-drawn bus, and disposes of the bandages that have robbed him of half his sight. He can see again, very well, actually, in spite of the rain. And his resolve is steeled: what he will do is say adieu forever to this poisoned, vulgar, cruel, hedonistic society rotting from the inside out, a society whose sole occupation consists in amassing useless things, slaughtering animals, and exterminating the soul.

A few stops later, at Alexanderplatz, a soaked Berliner is leaning against the wall of a building and eating—chewing, mesmerized—one of those bland bratwursts. The whole wretchedness of his people is written on his face. The unctuous, indifferent desolation, the gray lament of his bristly-cut hair, the oily specks of sausage between his crude fingers—one day he'll be painted like that, the German. Engelhardt, just as hypnotized, fixes him in his gaze as the omnibus rattles past through the wall of water. For a second it is as if a fiercely bright beam of light joins the two, one enlightened and one subordinate.

V

Now that we have endeavored to tell of our poor friend's past, we will skip a few short years, like an untiring, lofty seabird for whom crossing the time zones of our globe is of no consequence whatsoever, indeed, who neither notices nor reflects upon them, and visit August Engelhardt again where we left him a few pages ago: walking stark-naked on the beach—on his own beach, mind you—stooping here and there to collect an especially lovely shell and slip it into a wicker basket he has thrown over his shoulder.

The Time Statute of the German Empire, which was passed a good decade ago in Berlin and aptly went into effect on April 1 shortly before the turn of the century, ensured that a uniform hour could be read from the clocks of His Imperial Majesty's German subjects throughout the entire motherland. In the colonies, meanwhile, one told time according to the respective world time zone, while on the isle of Kabakon, in a sense, a time outside of time prevailed. Which is to say Engelhardt's clock, which he had placed on a piece of driftwood serving as a night table and wound with considerable regularity by means of a little key, had gone into arrears, temporally speaking, due to a single grain of sand; the granule had made itself comfortable within the clock between the spring and one of the hundred whirring cogs and, since it consisted of hard, pulverized corallite, was inducing a minute deceleration in the progression of Kabakonian time.

To be sure, Engelhardt did not notice this fact right away, nor even after a few days; in fact, a few years had to pass on Kabakon before the effect of the grain of sand made itself felt. The retardation was such that the clock did not lose even one second per day, and yet something gnawed and ate at Engelhardt, who expected something like a secure footing in space from a correct indication of time. He thought himself in the ethereal, cosmic present—should he have to forsake it, that would mean for him stepping out of time, which is to say, going mad.

That in faraway Switzerland another young vegetarian working in a patent office was compiling the theoretical underpinnings for his dissertation at precisely that moment, the contents of which but a few years later would turn upside down not only all of mankind's previous knowledge, but to a certain extent also the viewpoint from which one perceived the world and this knowledge, and even time, was unknown to Engelhardt.

When he contemplated whether his clock might not be running more slowly—it just seemed to him that way since he of course could not draw any comparisons to genuine, real time (the pendulum clock in the governor's residence over in Herbertshöhe, which one might look to as the standard time for the protectorate, had stopped due to the negligence of the staff while Hahl was convalescing in Singapore)—he suddenly

had the feeling he was going to fall backward; a painful, nag-
ging twinge in the left upper arm stabbed into him, just near
the heart, as if a stroke were actually felling him at his young
age. He distinctly saw the clock ticking away, his by-now-
finished rattan cot, and the mosquito net attached above it with
a coir rope. He was already falling into time when there appeared before his eyes, at first hazily, then in downright razor-
sharp focus, not only the canary-yellow and violet painted walls
of his childhood nursery, but the perfumed manifestation of
his mother, bending over him with the tip of her tongue stuck
out in worry and working over his hot forehead with an iced
cotton cloth. His mother could not only be seen; she could in
fact be felt, as if she were not long dead but present and infinite in the extreme—the boundless love that he felt for her
was indeed a cosmic, a divine sensation.

With gentle and calming words, his mother led him out
onto the terrace of his parents' home, and he became aware of
the rosebushes that grew down in the garden exuding their
heavy scent. It was the middle of the night. The summer crick-
ets were putting on their somniferous night concert when his
mother gestured toward the sky to show him that enormous
wheel of fire rotating above in the inky firmament. To the child
it looked like a savagely hungry, insatiable mouth devouring
everything.

Trembling with fear, he closed his eyes to the monstrous,
burning portent, hiding his face in his mother's bosom, the
cozy fullness of which instantly sent him falling deeper, which
is to say, further up, the current of time, until he came to lie
in a perambulator, immobile, as his infant body was not able
to turn or stretch out its little hands. And yet they were able

to feel the embroidered blanket with which he had been tucked in; in fact, he discerned the pale blue checkered pattern of a baby bonnet at the edge of his field of vision and saw above him the infinite forkings of a summery cherry tree under which someone had pushed the pram at midday. He heard ringing laughter, glasses clinked together, the barking of a dachshund. A pink blossom, marbled somewhat with midnight blue at the edges, glided down slowly and came to rest gently on his little face.

Unexpectedly, the queasy feeling that his body was floating overcame him. It was even earlier now. A soft surface that engulfed him, then the not-unpleasant impression that he was being drawn across pumice, over a whole volcanic expanse made of this very rock; for hours he floated a few inches above that expanse as if he were a helium balloon about to burst because of the rough surface of the stone, but then which laboriously manages to get free; there was a precipice, a pulling, a dragging. Finally he fell downward, a catastrophic plunge toward the earth, as if he himself were that blossom that had drifted down from the treetop. Then he awoke.

VI

During his stay on his island, Engelhardt had not only
lost several pounds, but had also grown wiry and
muscular; his skin was now a rich dark brown, and
his hair and beard, which he slathered with coconut oil every
morning, had become bright blond and golden from sun and
salt. Pursuant to his instructions, the oil his employees squeezed
on Kabakon was bottled in half-liter flasks on the mainland
and given an appealing label designed by the Herbertshöhe
postmaster, which showed Engelhardt's somewhat touched-
up, bearded profile. (The alternative—providing from the con-
gealed oil the base ingredient for Palmin cooking fat and the
margarine much in demand in Germany—was completely out
of the question for him, for ethical reasons; he would most certainly not supply his countrymen with vegetable oil in which to
sizzle their Sunday beefsteak.)

The oil-refining process Engelhardt paid for out of pocket
(or rather on credit from Queen Emma who was still, more
or less, smiling inscrutably), a somewhat doubled advance pay-
ment; one day that Kabakon Oil, which already lay stacked in

the Forsayth trading post packed in dozens of wooden crates, would surely find a buyer.

To this end, Engelhardt had established several very promising contacts in Australia, notwithstanding the fact that the letters he dispatched to Darwin, Cairns, and Sydney, as befell mailed advertisements all over the world, were briefly skimmed, then stacked, cut down the middle, and reused as coarse toilet paper; his letters in particular were employed in the staff privy of the accountant's office at a copper and bauxite mine not far from Cairns.

The writings that told of the therapeutic, thoroughly beneficial, and diverse possible applications of his Kabakon Coconut Oil, in Engelhardt's quite literary but somewhat awkward English, served the visitors to that Australian toilet only to a limited extent as entertaining reading while they did their business, as they had been perforated, cut, and separated at precisely those areas that would have enabled an unhindered read in complete sentences. Reassembled and reread with the hundreds of similar mailed advertisements, they no longer made any sense, of course. Thus, his letters wandered: scanned fleetingly, bereft of meaning, wadded up, and smeared with filth, they landed in a seepage pit on that gigantic, almost uninhabited continent to the south, which Engelhardt once visited with friendly intentions during the time remaining for him in the protectorate, but whose soldierly and coarse, mostly drunken inhabitants so disgusted him that after only a week and a half he boarded a mail steamer to return to New Pomerania.

The humiliating ends that befell his brochures remained concealed from Engelhardt. Had he found out, he would scarcely have decamped for Cairns; nor was he able to anticipate anything of the great calamity later to be dubbed the First World War. So it was only a premonition that afflicted him as he sauntered through the alleys of that Queensland gold mining town.

The following had happened to him: the wooden door of a public house had been pushed open, and a bearded colored man, a Pacific islander obviously, had fallen backward onto the dirt road, uttering a dull, grunting cry. The black man rolled over on his stomach in anguish and crawled toward Engelhardt; a throng of white Australians followed him out of the pub, whereupon he was cruelly beset with kicks until he could hardly ward off their brutal blows any further. He came to rest before Engelhardt with arm outstretched, bleeding and coughing and motionless. Recalling that he himself had once been so beaten, on that beach in East Prussia, Engelhardt knelt down and tried to lift the victim by the shoulders, but the white men, intoxicated nearly to the point of dehumanization, shoved him back brusquely, screaming, *Nigger lover!* and other despicable words.

One ought not treat a human being like that, Engelhardt said, growing furious, and all at once he sprouted wings of courage, and he stood up straight, a slight, rickety figure against six or seven rough gold panners. One now noticed his German accent, called him *dirty Hun*, and raised his fists to pummel him as well. Another held him back, saying that there would be war between Edward and the Kaiser soon enough anyway, and we'll teach 'em manners then, those bastard Germans. Finally, bawling out patriotic songs, they withdrew to the counter of the canteen bar whose publican, as was customary in those days in Australia, had diluted the brandy with gunpowder and cayenne pepper, to enhance the effect of the alcohol on the one hand and, on the other, to mask the repulsive taste of his hooch with a false, fiery note.

Aha, Engelhardt thought to himself. And, after putting a few shillings into the wounded colored man's still-outstretched hand, he made his way back to the boardinghouse room on the second floor of a clothier's, lay down on his bed with a sigh, and ruminated on the encounter. Could it not be that the subjects of His Britannic Majesty would one day annex the German protectorate just like that, were the war they had just prophesied to him, Engelhardt, actually to occur? Kaiser-Wilhelmsland, New Pomerania, and the smaller islands were defended by a mere handful of German soldiers, and it was precisely the extraordinary remoteness and irrelevance of the colony that had to seem tempting to a bellicose people, as the British doubtless were—much like raspberry cake would be to a hungry child. Engelhardt was, please note, unable to sense anything of the gigantic conflagration that would cover the globe a few years later, but from then on his senses were sharpened, his image of the British and young Australia altered forever by the encounter in Cairns: Would the sea become an Anglo-Saxon *Pacific*, would he be left to do as he pleased, on his Kabakon? Hardly. Wouldn't the little isle instead be annexed as well and his workers henceforth required to slave at his coconut palms for the English king? Then that free, that German, paradise would be finished.

While he was thinking this, next door, virtually tête-à-tête with him and separated only by a thin sheet of plywood that served as a divider for the boardinghouse rooms, lay a young man who was not dissimilar to Engelhardt in habitus and

countenance, likewise keenly contemplating, though his
thoughts at the moment did not revolve around a potential war
between the German Reich and Great Britain, but around yeast
paste. Halsey was a Seventh-day Adventist and baker, hailed
from the United States, also had a rather slight build, and was
developing ways to popularize natural foods. He had ended
up in Australia because the Christian-Adventist company for
which he worked had dispatched him there to sideline him,
on the one hand (for he was somewhat of an oddball), and, on
the other, to give him the opportunity to prove himself by
running riot, so to speak, over the sixth continent. Could be,
his masters in the far-off state of Michigan thought, could
be that young Halsey will make something of himself down
there among the kangaroos.

The Kellogg brothers had recently founded the Sanitas
Food Company in the United States, you see, and, with their
idea for producing so-called breakfast cereals palatable to
people, they were well on their way not only toward triggering
a small revolution in the eating habits of their countrymen,
but also toward becoming dizzyingly rich.

Young Halsey had asked the two brothers for an appointment, had appeared in their sparse, orderly office, and had
then thoroughly impressed upon them with the conviction
of an incensed fanatic that cereals were by no means the right
path to pure Adventist doctrine because ingesting them into
the body necessitated the addition of cow's milk—no one
wanted to eat dry cereal alone. But the milk that provided the
lubricant, as it were, was obviously an animal product; thus,
they must cease cereal production immediately and come up
with something new that could teach the American consumer

to be a vegetarian. *Good Lord*, off to Australia with him, the brothers thought, for they may have been pious adherents of their Adventist faith, but were simultaneously incorrigible, un-alloyed Yankees, confident of business as a raison d'être. And so Halsey traveled by steamer from San Francisco (which would be almost completely destroyed by an earthquake a very short time after his embarkation) across to Sydney and then to Cairns, and there he now lay, head to head with Engelhardt.

It is possible that both vegetarians felt each other's presence without being aware of it, as if the thin plywood panel between their heads were a kind of electrical conductor. Halsey was of course a genius, as was Engelhardt. It's just often the case that one person's genius is acknowledged in the world—his idea spreads and evolves like a well-told joke that isn't forgotten, like the virus of some disease—while the other's withers away under the saddest of circumstances. The Kellogg brothers, who had sent Halsey to the other end of the world, were con-vinced that their pupil's lines of thought to a certain degree must seem too radical for their time, but they were also un-doubtedly in love with him, in an avuncular sense. Still, they didn't want him on the same continent because he had criti-cized their foundations, had nibbled away at their morals, so to speak.

At any rate, on the following day the two sat at the same table in the breakfast room of the little boardinghouse, the windows of which looked out on a slightly sloping dusty street so that the sporadically recurring rain showers transformed it mostly into a muddy torrent. Frangipani blossoms would then come floating down the street, coming to rest before the boardinghouse, as they did today, for it was raining fiercely, and Engelhardt was brewing for himself with some care a cup of brown loam so as to spend the day reading in the boarding-house and then to prepare for his well-earned departure from Australia.

Halsey addressed him with interest, asking what sort of extract Engelhardt was mixing, and was informed that it was medicinal clay; if one couldn't get hold of the original product from Germany, one could use any soil, it contained all the minerals the body needed, for his visits to so-called civilization would suck those substances out of Engelhardt, and this was the only way he could stay healthy. But didn't Engelhardt live in civilization? Halsey wanted to know, whereupon the former replied with a dose of nonchalant pride that he was the leader and creator of the Order of the Sun and ran a coconut plantation in the German colonies north of Australia, so it depended on the definition of the word *civilization*. A truer word was never spoken, Halsey said, and requested permission to taste the medicinal clay. He was a strict vegetarian, he explained, and was always happy to try something new that didn't harm an animal in its production.

Halsey's idea, which he was now explaining to Engelhardt over a cup of the brown dust, was to develop a food paste that one could use as a healthy spread for bread—with a purely vegetable base, naturally—so as to cure young and old of the desire for meat through the flavor of the paste. The trick would be to blend this spread in such a way that the flavor would actually make one think one was in fact enjoying Liebig's popular Extract of Meat smeared on one's breakfast toast.

Cooked, preserved in a jar, and consisting of malt and yeast, the new foodstuff would be delectable and full of vitamins and create—and this was the actual idea (since, according to Halsey, behind every good world-altering thought there must be another, hidden thought)—a new type of person: a healthy, powerful vegetarian who did not have to answer for the blatant injustice of suffering animals. In short, Halsey wanted to reform his fellow man by outfoxing his palate. The dark brown yeast substance was to simmer in large vats in specially built factories the world over (for one would have to produce the paste in huge quantities), so he saw it in his mind's eye. On the one hand, Engelhardt was touched by Halsey's generous trust, though they had known each other for only about ten minutes (let's not count the night in which both, without knowing of each other, slept head to head and, so to speak, emanated into each other in their dreams). It was a proselytizing, vegetarian idea that this young Adventist was voicing, not dissimilar from Engelhardt's own conceptions.

But now he had been brooding for weeks about a suitable name and could not settle on one. He had here, if you please, a piece of paper with several options, most of them crossed out. Did Engelhardt perhaps have a revelatory idea? It should sound as healthful as possible, and with a harmonious succession of consonants and vowels. Please, Halsey said, could he not donate a name to his cause? Engelhardt urged the young American, quid pro quo, to travel with him to New Pomerania and try subsisting exclusively on coconuts for three months. During this time, he would then have the opportunity to give further thought to this spreadable condiment, its production (couldn't one perhaps also cook it from a copra paste?), as well as its marketing. On Kabakon they would arrive at a fitting name for this new product. Oh, yes, indeed, they would be naked together the whole time.

Halsey, to cut a long story short, refused everything, disconcerted and rather perturbed. He was sorry, but his vegetarianism had grown out of a quite puritanical tradition and would result in a pragmatic realism oriented, above all, toward capitalism. One's own body was not essential to his philosophy. Sure, it existed, but that was no reason to lie naked on a beach; surely no one could be persuaded by that. His counterpart seemed to him to be, if he might be permitted to say so, like all romantics, merely an egoist of a Schopenhauerian persuasion.

Engelhardt sat facing him very quietly for a spell while shredding up into tinier and tinier shreds Halsey's piece of paper with possible names on it and then in turn (for it is common knowledge that no people tear each other apart as exhaustively as those whose ideas are identical) began to reproach the poor Yankee. He was a Calvinist bore, and really, who was supposed to spread spiced paste on bread? He, Halsey, would see where he ended up—in the poorhouse; he'd fail with his phantasmagoria, which was basically premised only on exploitation, because he wanted to manufacture industrially and not discover what nature harmoniously offered him.

I see, I see, aha, Communist, idiot, Halsey blurted out, rising angrily, taking his hat from the table, and hurrying to the door. Traitor to our sacred vegetarian cause, Engelhardt called after him, and: Prudish, prematurely senile Philistine! This last, however, Halsey did not hear as he had long since disappeared into the crowd on the main road of Cairns, which was colored slate-gray by the rain, surfacing once or twice on one street corner or another until nothing more was left of him but the shredded paper with the ten or twelve potential names for the spread, which Engelhardt had tossed under the table, and which that evening—our hero having already departed—was swept up by the boardinghouse proprietor and tossed into the kitchen oven together with the package of medicinal clay Engelhardt had intentionally forgotten in his room. From now on, our friend swore to himself, he would live off coconuts exclusively. And those slips of paper that resembled black roses at the moment they went up in flames, their fluorescent edges gleaming whitish yellow? *Vegetarians Delite* could be read on those snippets, then a few names crossed out, among them *Veggie's Might*, *Yeastie*, and *Beast-Free*, and then, clear and distinct, underlined twice and marked with angular exclamation points, the word *Vegemite*.

Part Two

VII

L et us now speak about love. It was a grievous, rainy
return voyage. The ocean lay gray and leaden for a
depressing week; only just before the sighting of the
New Pomeranian coast did Engelhardt glimpse the sun he so
desired again. While still on the Herbertshöhe landing quay, he
was welcomed by his young boy Makeli, who had sailed over
from Kabakon to await the return of his master in the capital.
Engelhardt disembarked resignedly and unhappily. Marching
toward him, which is to say in the direction of the Imperial
Post ship, was a corpulent man in a white suit looking equally
grim. (It was Hartmut Otto, the awful bird dealer, who was
leaving New Pomerania again for the umpteenth time, en route
to Kaiser-Wilhelmsland since he had once more been cheated
most perfidiously out of a batch of bird-of-paradise feathers.)
They took no notice of each other.

Meanwhile, Makeli opened a hole-ridden umbrella over
Engelhardt's head to protect him from the piercing rain,
relieved him of the small carpetbag, and walked beside him

awhile in silence, sensing that his master was suffering from a great dejection. Pondering this or that means of cheering him up, he spontaneously recalled the young German waiting for Engelhardt in the Hotel Fürst Bismarck. He mustn't be so sad, Makeli smattered, after all he had a visitor from Germany. What, a visitor? Yes, a young blond man (who, incidentally, would not touch a bite of meat or fish) had been sitting here for over a week awaiting Engelhardt's return from Australia. Why, Makeli, boy, he now shouted, seizing him by the shoulders, why hadn't he said that right away? A visitor! What news!

Engelhardt left Makeli standing there smiling blissfully, while he raced down the street, flew through the puddles, side-stepped a weeping fig tree with vividly orange-red blossoms, skipped over the individual steps of the hotel veranda with a hop, and, breathing heavily, stopped before a freckled young man who in turn leapt up from the wicker sofa, tucked the blond forelock behind his ear, wiped his damp hands on his trousers, and introduced himself with a crooked grin as Heinrich Aueckens, vegetarian, from Heligoland. And that it was a colossal honor, a truly colossal honor, finally to stand face-to-face, so to speak, before the brilliant author of the book *A Carefree Future*. He had saved, paid for the voyage from his own pocket, and just left, without announcing himself by letter, of course, for which he begged pardon, but he had only ever left Heligoland once before, to study in Hamburg, so now he was here in any case and was tremendously glad, and he wanted to join the Order of the Sun, provided this was readily possible. The strawberry-blond Aueckens spoke without periods and commas, and Engelhardt sensed an immeasurable satisfaction rise up in his soul, like the invigoratingly

effervescent bubbles in a glass of mineral water, on account of
the so eagerly awaited visit.

In hindsight, it may be said that the exceedingly positive
first impression Engelhardt had gotten from his visitor was
heavily tinged by the feeling of his, Engelhardt's, loneliness,
and that he was moved, certainly, also by the recently experienced gruff rejection of his ideological edifice by the Yankee
Halsey, to immediately demolish, in Aueckens's presence, the
diffident defensive walls against people that he had so carefully erected during his childhood. This Aueckens, you see,
would soon turn out to be a first-class swine, which is why
even a few weeks later he was no longer among us; *il mangeait
les pissenlits par la racine*, as the French would say.

However did Aueckens learn of Kabakon's existence? our
friend wanted to know. Well, from a pamphlet by the nudist
Richard Ungewitter that he had received in Heligoland. In that
treatise, Engelhardt's experiment in the South Seas colonies had
been praised as an attempt to break through the intellectual
narrowness of Germany and establish a brave (albeit ultimately
utopian) new beginning under palm trees, far away from
the infirm machinery of a meaningless and ever-accelerating
society.

Engelhardt, who hadn't expected so much goodwill on
the part of Ungewitter (the two had severed epistolary contact
as a result of a severe difference of opinion that, in retrospect,
was probably based on a misunderstanding), bade his visitor
to have his luggage brought from the hotel room quickly, they
would ferry over together to Kabakon, he was to be the first
member of the Order of the Sun, so to speak, yes, yes, indeed,
Engelhardt would immediately and unceremoniously appoint

him a proper brother, they would then build a hut for him and, in general, do splendidly well together. Oh, there were otherwise no other members at all? Aueckens wanted to know, whereupon our friend proclaimed with a smile: not yet, one must be patient; the thought of living naked and free and only from coconuts was, though imperative, an idea that would need time to sink in among the civilized world. He paid Aueckens's hotel bill by signature, steered the young Heligolander down to the landing pier, and together they boarded the sailing canoe, which was navigated over to the isle by Makeli's steady hand.

By the very next day, the newcomer's palm-frond hut had been erected. And it was so very good to be able to converse, in German, about issues concerning German things. By no means had Engelhardt felt lonely, but the awareness that he could now share his thoughts with someone who possessed a similar horizon sent him into a rare euphoria. Aueckens had read Thoreau! They sat together on the beach, spoke about the political and ethical absurdity of the German government in having ceded East African Wituland, as well as the islands of Zanzibar, Lamu, and Pemba, for Heligoland a few years before, and shared the meat of several coconuts. It was overcast and windless. Before them in the sand, tiny crabs geared up to duel, keeping each other at bay in zigzags. Aueckens— one could most certainly not yet expect him to have already become a total cocovore—ate a few bananas as well, and Engelhardt gave a small toast in honor of his visitor. Elevating the coconut shell like a glass of Franconian wine, he thanked his new brother in spirit for having taken the long road here. Together they would soon be able to accept other new members into the Order of the Sun, leading by good example, for—and one could now hear them clink shell to shell while shouting, *Vivat!*—a superb idea will prevail all on its own, to be sure.

Humanity was not yet ready to accept Engelhardt's doctrine, however; humankind must first begin to transcend itself, and he called upon the following analogy (during the narration of which Aueckens, his head cocked slightly, scratched his forehead in thought): If while hunting around, for instance, an ant fell upon a piece of chocolate it had detected through the indeed astoundingly complex design of its antennae's sensorium, then this was an event comprehensible within the bounds of the formicine conceptual horizon and wholly natural to it. But if a human being entered into the equation, wanting to safeguard his chocolate, for example, by preventing that insect from notifying its peers so that together they might take possession of the sweet comestible, and if he thus hid the chocolate from the insect inside an icebox, then the ant (whose groping movements would grow continually slower and more unsure on account of the cold), still wandering around on that chocolaty surface, would have no possible way to figure out what was happening. The fact that it and the object of its desire had been put into a cold, hostile environment would lie entirely outside its conceptual apparatus; not even in a hundred thousand years could the ant understand the mechanism underlying the onset of its own demise by freezing, lacking as it does the ganglionic armamentarium, for example, to understand why it had ever become necessary for a culture to design a cabinet in which things may be kept cold by adding blocks of ice. It was similar for man, who wanted to understand his purpose on this planet; man's sensorium is simply not sufficient to grasp the whole background of the fact of his own existence. Were he able (but it would, as he said, lie in the realm of the completely impossible), then the veil of Maya would lift, and he would transcend his existence, would become godlike, quite analogously to the ant, who would finally break through to us, its immense deities, and our eternally opaque actions.

Aueckens, who didn't quite understand what Engelhardt was trying to explain with the ant and the chocolate, ceased listening the moment he noticed it was indeed a rather proper house that Engelhardt had built for himself here: an immaculate six-foot-wide veranda made of jackfruit tree timbers girded the whole structure. The walls of the interior rooms were decorated with pretty shells, a chessboard was set up and ready for play on a block of driftwood, a thoughtfully planted, lovely flower garden buzzing with vibrantly colored hummingbirds was about to bloom. There were windows with wooden louvers that could be properly sealed against weather and various wildlife, and if by evening the shutters were clapped shut, one felt safe and homey, a feeling that had pleasantly saturated Engelhardt when he had slept in his new dwelling the first night. Yes, let's be honest, he hadn't constructed it himself, but had sent for a skillful carpenter from Herbertshöhe, who erected the three-room home inside of a week and at his behest had even built for him a shrine from fragrant sandalwood on which Engelhardt had positioned an old carved wooden figurine so that its inscrutable gaze flowed through all the rooms of the house.

This fetish, with which a delegation of his workers had solemnly presented him at a small ceremony, was incidentally missing an ear in much the same way as Hotel Director Hellwig—the result of an amputation that a drunk missionary had performed a good twenty years ago while zealously attempting to familiarize the islanders of the Neu-Lauenburg archipelago with the Catholic faith by defiling their idols with an axe. The selfsame padre turned up later, having hardly slept off his inebriation, slain by his own axe. Left hanging on a tree afterward to be drained of blood, he was then portioned into small pieces on a ceremonial stone, the choicest of which were served steamed and wrapped in pandanus leaves to the owner of the figurine at the time, an influential chieftain. That grandee, who most certainly did not lack for a sense of humor, insisted on having the ear of the missionary for dessert, roasted crispy on a wooden skewer—quid pro quo, so to speak.

These rather bestial circumstances (which also dated back quite a while, in fact) cast a morbid shadow over Engelhardt's existence in a paradise where everything was actually going according to his wishes; the first adept had arrived from Germany, the natives were not only pacified and turned halfway vegetarian, but also tempered with benevolence and a willingness to work. His crates of books, which had remained intact and undamaged by the humid adversities of numerous voyages, were brought to shore by the sailing canoes, finally unpacked, and his sacrosanct tomes were first stacked on their sides against the walls of his little house and then, by and by, following an exact alphanumeric system, ordered in modern-seeming shelves constructed specially for this purpose. Kabakon's inhabitants said privately that Engelhardt possessed what they called *mana* (and what we Europeans sometimes know simply as *mazel*), and he was, for a short time, happy, plain and simple. The first dark clouds, however, were already advancing, and briskly at that, as we shall now see.

It had sometimes seemed to him as a child that another world where everything had panned out differently in a bizarre, but wholly reasonable and compelling way existed alongside this one. Entire continents arose, alien and unfamiliar, from oceans unseen before, the trace of their coastlines running rough and unmapped over a planet illuminated by a double moon. On broad, uninhabited plains blanketed in soft wild grass, cities towered aloft steeply; their builders had never drawn upon the sequence of our architectural history, and the Gothic remained as unknown to them as the buildings of the Renaissance. Instead they followed their own completely alien aesthetic stipulations, which dictated that towers and walls, at breakneck heights, were to be built in such a way and no differently. Moored balloons in every conceivable shape and color peopled the skies over those cities, which for their part were brightened at night by colorful beacons. Gentle animals similar to our deer grazed before the gates without fear of being captured and eaten by the inhabitants. Only humans had never appeared to him, not once. Sometimes he still saw this world in his nightly dreams, and upon awakening, he yearned to return there with excruciating longing.

In the morning, Engelhardt marched down the beach and, knocking theatrically at Aueckens's palm-frond hut with raised knuckles, he woke his comrade-in-arms with the of course heavily German-accented words: *In the hollow Lotos-land to live and lie reclined, on the hills like Gods together, careless of mankind.* Aueckens started, rose naked from his bed of sand, rubbed the sleep from his eyes, cleared his throat laboriously, and, sweeping the intractable lock from his forehead, continued Tennyson's famous poem: *Then some one said, "We will return no*

more"; And all at once they sang, "Our island home is far be-
yond the wave; we will no longer roam."

Though touched by the solemn stanzas, they snorted with
boyish laughter, clapped each other on the back in greeting,
interjecting that one need only replace *Lotos* with *Cocos*, then
both ran naked and huffing into the surf. Strangely enough,
Aueckens grasped Engelhardt's hand in the process; only reluc-
tantly did the latter allow it, since he felt it to be disrespectful
and false. In fact, Aueckens had expected he would be allowed
to sleep in Engelhardt's little house as a guest of the order; for
now he was provided with the somewhat secluded palm-frond
hut that had served our friend as his first lodgings on Kabakon. Engelhardt had decided on this arrangement after a conversation with Aueckens during a morning stroll on the beach
in which Aueckens declared that, for him, part of freedom of
spirit was also freedom of sexuality. How did he mean this?
Engelhardt inquired. Well, the young visitor had answered, to
put it bluntly, he was partial to love between men, he had tried
it once with a Frisian farm girl, but quickly realized that he
could venerate only the male body. The vegetarian Plutarch
himself had understood love between men as an expression of
the highest civilization; throughout history, odes to boys had
been written, the Philistine reinterpretation of which could
only be explained by a centuries-old prudery, and the very
breach of this fact Aueckens had made his aim. Homosexuality was the intrinsic, the authentic state of man, his love of
women, by contrast, an absurd erratum of nature.

In August of last year, after an extended excursion through
the Heligoland uplands where the seagulls floated motion-
lessly over the cliff near Hoyshörn like white stones in the

wind, Aueckens had, while lounging in a teahouse, spotted a young man whose protruding ears, dark Cimmerian eyes, and peculiar paleness just did not seem to fit in. It was as if that appallingly thin schoolboy sitting with his uncle at a table and nibbling on a piece of rock candy were the most alien element imaginable in the composition of the island. This little stranger made him wild with lust, Aueckens reported to his mentor, Engelhardt, who in turn nodded sympathetically, while attempting with some difficulty to conceal from Aueckens his aversion toward such openly declaimed homosexuality.

So at any rate, after Aueckens had intimated to him with looks and subtle nods that he ought to excuse himself from his uncle and follow him outside, the young man walked into the summer air, where, in reality, the following had transpired: The boy had taken but a few steps before Aueckens's strong hands had pressed the slender shoulders of the young urbanite against the exterior wall of the teahouse and he had tried to stick his tongue in his ear while his hand had fumblingly made for the front of the boy's trousers (like, the groped boy felt, a hairy, spiderlike insect). Repulsed, the boy had pushed him away with a brief yelp of indignation, and at this moment it had struck Aueckens that the aim of his amorous advances had emitted a strong odor.

After the lad had fled back to his uncle in the inn, he, Aueckens, had known why; to wit, he had been a Jew, a hirsute, sallow, unwashed, Levantine emissary of things un-German (the so-described schoolboy, meanwhile, a vegetarian himself, wrote a card later that same day to his sister in Prague: his cough had gotten better at the ocean, his uncle was showing him the sights, now they were shipping off to Norderney, it was barren here, but impressive, the residents of the rocky island, however, coarse and mentally retarded).

Engelhardt, scraping all the while with his toes in the sand, had listened to the story with increasing consternation. When Aueckens closed with the words that he had been rebuffed because his victim had been a Jew, Engelhardt tried to pick a scab from his shin and secretly ingest it (an incipient infection? or had he cut himself somewhere?) and then began yawning deeply, saying that they could chat more tomorrow.

Later in bed he reflected on the matter. The sickle of the moon hung cheese-colored over the ocean. What a horribly disagreeable person this Aueckens was. Engelhardt did not share that emergent trend of demonizing the Semitic, which with his writings and turgid, strange music the dreadful Richard Wagner had if not initiated, then made socially acceptable everywhere. Our friend loved the music of Satie and Debussy and Mendelssohn-Bartholdy and Meyerbeer.

What had triggered his quarrel with the nudist Richard Ungewitter, whose dubious treatise Aueckens had brought to him, had not been some misunderstanding, Engelhardt now remembered, but those very same hate-soaked allegations against the Jews, which worsened with every letter. Passing judgment on people on the basis of their race was to be strictly repudiated. Period, end of story. There was no discussion to be had about it. As a matter of fact, he had to get a piano. Thoughts circled like a child's carousel. Only how would one keep sand from getting into the piano's action? He hadn't seen Makeli for some time; hopefully nothing had happened to him. A nightbird screeched. A demon blew into an ivory horn. The Scythian kings kept blind slaves whom they employed to process milk. There, in the land of Gog and Magog, wherefore darkness prevailed. Finally, as the morning was already dawning, the nightmare broke away, and Engelhardt fell into a gentle sleep under the veil of his mosquito net, which had trapped those phantasmagorias.

Then that day looms, sunny and hot. We see both men walking naked on the beach. Engelhardt notices how Aueckens ogles him. He shows no inclination to avert his gaze from Engelhardt's private parts. If Engelhardt runs ahead for a while, he feels Aueckens's gaze resting on his backside. He feels watched, penetrated, reduced to his sex. Henceforth Engelhardt wears the waistcloth again on their walks together, Aueckens goes nude, the conversation proceeds haltingly: no more Tennyson.

We see the young Makeli roaming across the island with the thought of catching a magnificent green bird to give to Engelhardt, because his master, good old Makeli thinks, still seems so lonely in spite of the visitor from Germany. He is scouring the skies and the tops of the palm trees for the longed-for bird when, rather suddenly, the unpleasantly athletic, freckled Aueckens steps out of the copse on the right and grabs him, daubs a spot of lubricant from a bottle of Kabakon Coconut Oil brought for this purpose onto the tip of his erect penis with his thumb and index finger, and in a grove of palms rapes the boy, who shrieks like a wounded animal. Birds startle up, circle, cannot come to rest.

We do not meet Aueckens again until he is dead, lying facedown on the ground and naked, with a shattered skull;

some gelatinous brain matter has leaked out. Flies carouse on
the still-lustrous wound at the back of his head, which simply
will not dry—it seems as if it were still pulsing, as if a tiny bit of
life had not yet been extinguished and were still present at that
spot. Makeli is nowhere to be seen, Engelhardt but a shadow.
By evening rain comes and washes away the blood.

Whether Engelhardt beat the anti-Semite over the head
with a coconut himself, or whether Aueckens, wandering in that
same grove of palms where he had violated young Makeli, was
accidentally struck dead by a falling fruit, or whether the native
boy's hand raised a stone in self-defense—this tends to vanish
in the fog of narrative uncertainty. We can only be quite sure
of the fact that by the impact of a hard round object, Aueckens found his way from this world to Ultima Thule, from the
sun-drenched, palm-lined beach over into the cold, shadowy
realm of ice. And since Aueckens, who had hardly sojourned in
the protectorate for six weeks, was buried in the German Cemetery in Herbertshöhe quickly and without ceremony and was
neither missed nor mourned, oblivion soon blanketed the fact
that our friend may perhaps have committed a murder. Fatali-
ties of such a kind simply happened in the colonies; in New
Pomerania's civil registry, a scant entry is to be found. A crimi-
nal investigation never occurred because the governor's deputy
decided a coconut plummeting down from a tree had hit Aueckens, thus making it an accident, and so he did not even dispatch
a representative to Kabakon to investigate the matter.

Had someone from the capital come, he would have had
to interrogate Makeli, for young Makeli, his honor salvaged
by Aueckens's death, was a witness to the episode—but nothing, absolutely nothing, is to be learned from him. The boy's

love for his master, August Engelhardt, grew ad infinitum thereafter, however, and the evening reading sessions, which had been canceled due to the sodomite's short visit, were now finally resumed. There was indeed no shortage whatsoever of interesting books—after Dickens, it was time for the spirited tales of E.T.A. Hoffmann.

VIII

O
nly once more did Engelhardt leave the Bismarck Archipelago before everything went down the drain, so to speak. He had begun to consider the possibility of no longer paying his debts because he of course had to begin rejecting the complex, pernicious structure of the capitalist system somewhere. A pen friend from Heidelberg who led the more-than-gloomy existence of a completely impoverished adjunct scholar at that famous university confided in him that there was a young German man quite near Engelhardt who had set about translating into reality a similar—at least intellectually related—world of thought, someone living on a Pacific island, too, emulating the anorexia mirabilis of one Blessed Columba of Rieti who ingested no nourishment, none at all, except the golden light of the sun. The person in question lived on the Fiji Islands, and wasn't that just a stone's throw away, and wouldn't Engelhardt like to visit there one day?

Well, now, highly interesting, Engelhardt thought, putting aside the letter and opening a somewhat dated but still quite usable atlas; Fiji lay as far away from the protectorate as Australia, albeit not in a southerly, but in an easterly direction. One would perhaps be able to travel by way of the New Hebrides. As his fingers traced the route across the blue-inked expanse of the Pacific Ocean, he shoved his right thumb into his mouth and sucked on it, unawares. This quirk had been driven out of him with heavy beatings when he was a child, and he had discovered it for himself again, *herkos odonton*, as the tried-and-true expedient of a technique of meditation known only to him. Whenever he sank into a void within himself, sucking his thumb allowed him to block out the environment almost completely, indeed, to withdraw to such a degree that he was protected from each and every irritation surging onto the shores of his consciousness as if from a voracious moth by a particularly finely woven mosquito net.

And so he put on his lap-lap, filled a sack with coconuts, sailed over to Herbertshöhe, and inquired after the arrival of the French mail boat to Port Vila, which coincidentally, as if his journey were indeed part of some cosmic plan, was to reach New Pomerania the next day (the Messageries Maritimes ran this route only twice per year exactly). He borrowed the fare for the cheapest ticket from the postmaster, who was always well disposed toward him, and embarked the following day, barefoot, on the *Gérard de Nerval*, unrolling his coir mat on the quarterdeck in the very same manner as those natives who, bashful and almost invisible, had to undertake a voyage aboard the great ships of the white men. His intention to slip aboard the *Gérard de Nerval* secretly so as not to have to touch any more impure money he had quickly discarded.

The few Frenchmen who did not completely ignore him thought him an artist wallowing in primitivism, a German

version of their Gauguin, ergo a thoroughly laughable figure
who—and here it became apparent that the Gallic petit bourgeois was capable of displaying greater tolerance than his
dark, Teutonic counterpart hailing from the other side of the
Rhine—nevertheless had a raison d'être, even if it were only to
see the crusty old burgher validated (that is to say, themselves).
Frenchmen per se sympathized quite instinctively with figures
at the margins of society. Even if they feared innovation, in-
sofar as it heralded a superior culture and the concomitant
obsolescence of their own mediocrity, they did not necessarily
stand inimically opposed to it, but instead regarded it with
expectance, amusement, and by all means with curiosity, too.
The French might have been glaring snobs in their autistic elegance, but since their culture defined itself through language,
through *la francophonie*, and not as in Germany through the
mythical rustlings of affinity by blood, they appeared more het-
erogeneous than the Germans, for whom there were no shades
of difference, no nuances, few gradations of tone.

Engelhardt did not even do them the favor of dining in the
salons, instead waiting until darkness fell and then consuming
a few coconuts from his sack. Afterward, he lay lengthwise in a
corner of the quarterdeck, looked out onto the expansive black-
green sea mirroring the moonlight, and, after a few hours of
monotonous staring, gave himself over to his dreams, which
had recently seemed to him ever more menacing and eerie.

Thus he did not hear the songs of the passengers who sent
champagne-heavy chansons drifting off across the Pacific Ocean
deep into the night, indeed almost until daybreak; on the fes-
tively lit *Gérard de Nerval*, the drinking was even more ram-
pant than it had been once on the *Prinz Waldemar*. The only

intoxicant running through Engelhardt's body, though, was that milky-clear virginal honey, that opal squeezed into liquid form, *Cocos nucifera*. And if he had long ago decided never again to allow himself to be inspirited by alcohol, the coconut milk put him in such a state of arousal that he seemed to perceive, even while sleeping, that his blood was being successively replaced by said coconut milk. Indeed, it seemed to him as if it were no longer red, animal lifeblood streaming through his veins, but the fundamentally more highly developed vegetal nectar of his ideal fruit, which would one day enable him to transcend his current stage of evolution. It cannot be said with certainty whether his diet or even his increasing loneliness was to be regarded as the cause of his gradually budding psychological disorder; at the very least, however, the exclusive consumption of coconuts exacerbated an irritability that had always existed in him, an unrest in the face of certain, putatively unalterable, vexing external circumstances.

Now, while Engelhardt was traveling eastward on the French steamer, it was decided, after a very brief discussion over in Herbertshöhe, to dismantle the capital of German New Guinea and rebuild it not twelve miles farther up the coast, still in Blanche Bay, at a place called Rabaul, in close proximity to the volcano. The entrance to the harbor was in danger of filling up with sand sooner or later, there perhaps being some undersea current that washed tons of silt into the bay every day. At any rate, Herbertshöhe ceased to exist from one day to the next. Arrangements were made to carry all the buildings through the jungle; they had been neatly disassembled, piled in stacks of planks and boxes of nails, and furnished with precise blueprints for reconstruction. An antlike procedure orchestrated conscientiously by Hahl's deputy played out between the old and new capital, a busy coming and going during which two indigenous porters were struck and killed by falling trees and one unfortunate soul was bitten on the bare foot by a death adder because he had not wanted to drop an antique piece of furniture he was to carry through the jungle to Rabaul. The German ladies drove with the lone automobile. Everything was rebuilt nimbly and with great care just as it had stood in Herbertshöhe: the two hotels, the governor's residence, the trading posts, the piers. Even a glorious new wooden church, which looked exactly as the one just dismantled (except for a portrait of Kaiser Wilhelm II, hung mistakenly with his face to the wall), was erected and quickly consecrated by the local pastor. Emma's Villa Gunantambu, too, was relocated to Rabaul; still, many were initially unable to grow accustomed to going down Chinatownward to the left rather than right, and they missed trees that had stood in particular places—indeed, it was exceedingly disorienting.

En route, Engelhardt very nearly ran into Christian Slütter, with whom he had once played chess in the Hotel Fürst Bismarck in Herbertshöhe. After the *Gérard de Nerval* had moored in Port Vila and Engelhardt had transferred himself onto a British postal ship bound for the Fiji Islands, Slütter, though it was not really consistent with his character (or perhaps precisely for that reason), had brawled in front of a dive with an American Baptist who had rudely kicked aside a native standing in his way. The preacher had been a snake-eyed six-footer in a dark, heavily stained robe with hands like steam hammers. One punch hit Slütter in the face on the left, one on the right. Dazed, he sailed to the ground. It was nothing to speak of, just a brawl like any other in a harbor town, but for the fact that the man of God, in a flying rage, drew from his boot a stiletto to stick into the belly of the groaning German lying on the ground. Just then, an iron rod came whistling from the side; the native whom Slütter had wanted to defend had stepped in, picked it up off the ground, and swung it around for all he was worth; it caught the Yankee behind his right ear. Slütter escaped the tumult by crawling behind a building and waiting until the local gendarmes who had come running had withdrawn again, hauling off the native offender. In the meantime, Slütter had dragged into his hideout the irrefutable proof of guilt, that fatal iron with the bloody clumps of the preacher's hair, lain himself down on it, and had then fallen asleep, exhausted, where we shall let him be for the moment, until he surfaces again.

At first glance, the little town of Suva on Fiji resembled Herbertshöhe (or rather its new likeness, Rabaul), though it was populated by hustlers, drunkards, pirates, Methodists, beachcombers, and other unsavory characters who had chosen this little British colony Fiji, from all the islands in the Pacific Ocean, as the place to make their trouble—God alone knows why.

The light-eater and practitioner of prana, Erich Mittenzwey from Berlin, had meanwhile settled on a nameless neighboring Fijian isle—he had been receiving pilgrims and disciples for months—and when Engelhardt alighted there, it seemed to him as if he were looking in a fun-house mirror at his own future colony of cocovores. He was bidden welcome, and, in the fallacious assumption that he was likely a devotee of Mittenzwey's, he was assigned a place to sleep in one of the rattan huts that had been erected by the dozen along the little bay.

Everything seemed strictly organized and arranged in the German manner; Engelhardt watched with amazement as a young man swept the beach, lost in thought.

Mittenzwey himself, not especially emaciated, made his appearance after midday; he took a seat on a throne-like structure fashioned of bamboo, disrobed except for a kerchief-sized cloth that covered his private parts, and under various contortions that Engelhardt interpreted as freely improvised yogic poses began to open his mouth wide, snapping like a carp so as to absorb sunlight into his person. The small crowd of pilgrims sitting at his feet marveled, and they threw themselves to the ground, imitating him, attempting to drink the sunbeams. Engelhardt, who felt a fathomless fury rise up in him, took a seat in the sand next to a young Indian (Mittenzwey had again disappeared into his hut) and asked him what exactly was going on here.

Well, for over half a year, the fakir Mittenzwey had ingested neither food nor water—only the essence of light. This had been common practice in Europe during the Middle Ages, but Mittenzwey had refined the discipline with Indian philosophy here on the Fiji Islands, which were populated in large part by descendants of the wage laborers who had immigrated from northern India. In principle, the point was to store up prana, that stuff that surrounds us, by means of certain breathing techniques: in short, to transform ether into nutrients. It of course required a maximum of concentration and willpower, not everyone would be successful, one needed to enter a trance using certain meditative techniques acquired over many years for the world spirit (which conveniently rode on the light rays) to begin to permeate the body. Yes, and in order to pay homage to him, one brought the master gifts of money, watches, and jew-elry, which he stored openly in his hut to visualize for himself at all times the transience of the world and its vain frippery.

Engelhardt had heard enough; he hadn't come across such skulduggery in ages. He arose, walked up the beach to Mitten-zwey's dwelling, shoved the rattan curtain aside without knocking or otherwise announcing himself, and entered that most sacred sanctuary of the Berlin fakir. Mittenzwey and a dark-skinned elder Indian were sitting at a little table and shot up like children caught red-handed, sweeping into the corner, aghast, the various bowls with rice, fruits, and chicken drum-sticks; then the two collapsed in a heap. Mittenzwey resignedly buried his forehead in his hands, the Indian stood up and wiped his mouth, and at this moment Engelhardt realized that it was Govindarajan who stood before him, the treacherous Tamil who had once, years ago, lured him into a dark den on the is-land of Ceylon and then robbed him of his money.

During the brief moment of mutual recognition, Mitten-zwey fell to his knees; the German must not betray them to his disciples, for heaven's sake, it looked worse than it really was, they had without a doubt displayed fraudulent intentions, but no one had been forced to give them their valuables, this had simply begun one morning, then the arriving devotees had brought more and more presents, and giving them back had become impossible, plain and simple. Then Mittenzwey offered Engelhardt two handfuls of jewelry and valuable watches from a chest hastily pulled up and opened, and Govindarajan asked what sort of odd splotches Engelhardt had there, down on his legs.

Ignoring as much as possible Govindarajan's repulsive, smug visage and the precious objects so shamelessly offered, Engelhardt asked Mittenzwey what he really wanted to know: Was the whole practice of inhaling prana really only quackery, or was it in fact possible to ingest nothing but light? (The dishes strewn about the floor did rather suggest the former.) The Berlin fakir, who was, deep down, not a villainous person, replied meekly that he had tried fasting for approximately twenty-four hours and had very quickly reached the limits of his body. The worst thing, of course, had been the thirst, but he had known then with certainty that no one could live for months merely on the gifts of the sun.

Oh, rubbish, Engelhardt practiced nothing less, he ate of the fruit of the sun, and had done so for years, he replied with satisfaction, and they could keep their schlock, he was not going to reveal anything, they were merely a sad sight to behold, the Tamil and Mittenzwey, but he now knew that henceforth not only would he have to surround himself solely with Pure Doctrine, he would also have to set about attracting devotees whom he could face on equal footing—he, who suffered from the fact that no one came to visit him on his own island, he who would have liked to have had a friend, a fellow utopian. But when he saw what sort of shoddy cretin Mittenzwey had at his side there, he knew that being alone would always be preferable to this Byzantine underhandedness, to this pathetic house of lies here on Fiji. Phooey, he said, and adieu, and then he stepped out without honoring that sad hoodlum Govindarajan with even so much as the thought of a glance. It wouldn't have been acceptable to demand his money back from him since he had decided never to touch money again, even though he doubtless could well have used it to chip away at the mountain of debt he had amassed over in the protectorate.

Govindarajan, who of course had spent the money many years ago, cackled like a malevolent goat, for he had indeed recognized the spots on Engelhardt's legs. Then came a disparaging hand gesture; he whispered to Mittenzwey that one needn't bother with that one there any longer, he was on his way to the underworld anyway, their lucky streak, however, was far from over, and he proceeded to tidy up the hut again, throwing the chicken bones and the rice into the fire pit and covering everything with ashes and sand, still smirking to himself.

His thumb now in his mouth more often than he himself thought right, Engelhardt sailed back, this time as a stowaway on a German cruiser of the Imperial Navy, the SMS *Cormoran*, which had taken on coal and freshwater in Suva Harbor. He had hidden himself in one of the lifeboats covered in tarpaulin and taken a few coconuts with him to ward off hunger and thirst. He passed his water by urinating into an empty coconut shell, which he then slung at night through the slightly tented tarpaulin on the seaward side, far out into the darkness of the ocean. To be sure, not all that much would have happened to him had he been discovered—it was a German ship, after all—but in those days it did happen that boat crews from other nations were not especially gingerly in their treatment of stowaways—Frenchmen, Russians, and Japanese tossed the unfortunate souls overboard without a second thought, as if one were in the middle of that most crude eighteenth century and not in our conscientious twentieth. Engelhardt was forced to think of the poor bastards floating on the ocean's surface watching their respective ships sail away, death by thirst or exhaustion imminent, without even the faintest hope, thousands upon thousands of miles of ruthless sea all around, and a shudder came over him, and he shoved his thumb ever more firmly in his mouth.

After two weeks of a completely uneventful, sunlit voyage, the *Cormoran* anchored in Blanche Bay, and Engelhardt quit his safe hideout, satisfied with the success of his gratis excursion. In the general bustle of the warship's arrival, he mingled with the crowd on the jetty and suddenly took a powerful fright when he noticed that he was not in his trusted Herbertshöhe at all, but that the houses, palms, and avenues seemed to have been displaced in an extremely jarring way. He grew so disoriented that he felt as if he were going to faint and a gigantic force were sucking him into a tiny hole where he would then be disassembled into atoms.

Stumbling, he shoved his way past the white-clad onlookers, their facial features swimming before him. There was the church, my goodness, only it was standing the wrong way around. He tore at his beard with both hands. Over there was the Imperial Post Office, but across the way the Forsayth trading post that had still been there a few weeks ago was missing, while now, damn it, it was standing next to the Hotel Fürst Bismarck.

Beseechingly, he approached this or that passerby: Please would someone tell him what had happened here? But they evaded him; the sight of this obviously deranged long-haired man dressed in only a lap-lap was too bizarre. Hotel Director

Hellwig, who was strolling toward the governor's residence conversing with an officer from the *Cormoran*, gave a start at the sight of the severely emaciated owner of the Kabakon plantation who was flailing about like a grotesque revenant in the middle of the avenue. He left the officer where he was and tried to explain to Engelhardt that the city had been relocated— Jesus, Mary, and Joseph, hadn't anyone told him?—but the latter could only stare at the hotel owner's missing ear, as if there, from that cartilaginous atavism, could be divined the place into which his grip on reality had gradually vanished. He produced not a single German word, but in a continuous stammer, and finally speaking in tongues, abandoned Hellwig, who in fact felt rather sorry for the little fellow, and walked down to the beach to look for his sailing canoe, which would bring him back to his own sanity-restoring island.

IX

In the middle of the fourth or fifth year, an out-of-tune
piano came to Kabakon, as had been hoped for so long
ago. It came in the nurturing company of a man who had
announced himself in three letters, each arriving shortly after
the one before it, with exalted and anointed formulations: Max
Lützow, violin and piano virtuoso from Berlin, director of the
Lützow Orchestra (which had been named for the blond-
haired rake), ladies' man, though of course the last bit was not
in the letters.

Lützow was burned out, which is to say, washed up; he was
tired of civilization and carried with him a terrifying assem-
blage of half-imagined sicknesses of which he had unreserv-
edly made use in order to cloak the malaise of his everyday
German life in a shroud of hypochondria. He suffered by turns,
depending on weather conditions and how he was feeling, from
asthma, rheumatism, whooping cough, migraines, ennui, chills,
anemia, consumption, tinnitus, osteoporosis, back pain, worms,
sensitivity to direct sunlight, and chronic rhinitis.

Lützow was of course perfectly healthy, as every specialist

in Berlin had been telling him for years, and so, for want of a medical confirmation of his escalating symptoms, visible only to himself, he had undergone a series of newfangled cures, chief among them hypnosis. When the costly visits to Charlottenburg's mesmerists yielded few results—indeed, gave him neither relief nor special insight into the causes of his alternating ailments—he had even undertaken a trip to Vienna at the recommendation of a Jewish cellist friend of his to ask Dr. Sigmund Freud, who practiced there in the Ninth District, to dissect his brain, so to speak, in an evaluation.

But the latter had turned him away after a very short conversation; the Berlin musician's minor hysteria had seemed too pitiful and uninteresting to the famous neurologist, and so the former, on the very same evening that he arrived in Vienna, was sitting on the train back to Berlin, mentally putting a checkmark next to Dr. Freud's name, and resolving to become a vegetarian immediately, since the suffering of animals in slaughterhouses seemed to resonate morphologically, more or less through the intake of food, deep within the echo chamber of his own body.

Lützow tossed the ham sandwich purchased from the train station buffet out the window of the departing train, sank into an unsettled twilight sleep due to the steady clatter of the railway, and, having changed trains in Prague and arrived in the early evening in Berlin, immediately obtained for himself in a bookstore at the Zoological Garden a whole crate of freethinking, contemporary literature on the topic of vegetarianism. Included in it—Lützow was immediately ensnared as a bee buzzing astray that lands in sticky resin—was the treatise with the euphonious title *A Carefree Future*. The bookseller had mumbled something about New Guinea, and right away Lützow had appeared at the Berlin branch of Norddeutscher Lloyd and, in a thoroughly euphoric state of mind accompanied by the promise of offbeat escapades, purchased a ticket to the South Seas.

Engelhardt, who was just then finally cutting his toenails after many months of their sun-induced growth (for this he used paper scissors a great deal too large for the purpose, which he had bought from the Herbertshöhe postmaster for the outrageous sum of one mark eighty-five pfennigs)—they had grown out several inches from his feet such that he had tripped several times on exposed tree roots and larger conches—was sitting on the little wooden staircase that led up to his veranda and observing with bemused curiosity the contortions of the indigenous men, dripping with sweat, who endeavored to heave the piano from the steam launch onto two canoes and bring it to the shore of his bay without getting their feet wet. They were toiling quite dexterously, but the weight of the instrument was too large for the canoes, which almost put the bobbing boats in danger of capsizing. Max Lützow stood among the men—gesticulating, shirtless, his head bright red— and conducted the preposterous process of unloading the piano.

While Engelhardt was still quickly going over the middle toe of his left foot with the scissors (he nibbled off his fingernails; this was the only animal protein he ingested from time to time, and we would simply forgive him this little form of auto- anthropophagy and let it go entirely unmentioned if it didn't prematurely bespeak a certain symbolic significance), the men finally pulled and dragged the piano up onto the beach, its feet now digging into the wet sand, leaving deep furrows that reminded Engelhardt of the trail of a giant tortoise that has left the protective sea to lay her eggs.

He discarded this thought, which seemed to him in the moment of thinking it curiously indecent, laid the expensive scissors at the outer edge of the shell- and driftwood-bedecked veranda, covered his loins with the waistcloth that had previously served him as a receptacle for the clipped toenails (upon sight of the virtuoso, whom he awaited with joyful skepticism, he forbade himself his secret habit, likely borne of boredom, of using his collected toenails as a source of nutrition, too), and walked down to the shore, his right arm stretched aloft, to greet his guest from Germany, who had by then sunk into the sand, weary and depleted. In the meantime, a shadow crept around the house and, with a quick, sure hand, stole the scissors flashing there in the sunlight—it's to be assumed that it was Makeli.

Lützow's arrival had caused quite a stir in Rabaul, especially among the few German women who expected from the prominent musician at the very least a revitalization of their soirees, which were characterized by boredom, catty remarks, and the same conversations repeated ad infinitum—or at best the possibility of a little flirting. Evening after evening, the handsome young Berliner in his white flannels was more lugged than bidden to the German Club's piano—in order to entertain those planters and their wives convened there with a repertoire culled from clichés of fashionable music. They demanded of him maudlin standards, and he played everything as desired on the horrible-sounding instrument, including Donizetti and Mascagni and above all that gooey Bizet.

It had quickly gotten around, however, that Lützow intended to settle on Kabakon with August Engelhardt, which led to a rise in esteem for Engelhardt and a simultaneous drop in esteem for Lützow. They tried to dissuade him with all possible means. That fellow over on his isle was out of his mind; he lived—it could hardly be believed, they told him—by turns from nuts and flowers and was naked all day long. Mentioning this fact nevertheless led to a slight flush among the women, which they attempted to camouflage by theatrically wagging their fans. From their bosoms rose the scents of tuberoses, verbena, and musk, which diffused like invisible ground fogs and wafted fragrantly, pregnant with insinuation, through the salons of the club. But he really must stay here in Rabaul, where it was fun and civilized—in the next few months, they were even expecting a Marconi device, and couldn't he just play *Carmen* once more, just one more time?

Lützow was driven to the edge of despair: here he had traveled thousands of miles only to find himself in exactly the same situation he had fled. The provinciality of Rabaul was many times more pronounced than that of Berlin; he could just as well have gone to Cannstatt or Buxtehude. There, the very same matrons would have leaned over him in their unfashionably flared dresses with yellowed armpits, from whose décolletés, wreathed with Madeira lace, overripe breasts billowed like leavened dough, sugary glasses of liqueur in their beringed hands, and would have made the same suggestive comments about his ambidextrousness; only here it was infinitely hotter and many times more insipid. Queen Emma alone, who kept away from the German Club and its pretentious provinciality with good reason, would have been able to snap him out of his despondency. But alas, the two were due to meet at a point in time when it was, by all accounts, already too late.

Following a sudden intuition, Lützow interrupted his playing one evening, drew aside Hotel Director Hellwig, who joined in the amusements at the club every evening, to a two-person table out on the veranda, and asked him to facilitate the purchase of that piano. He was offering three hundred—oh, what the hell—four hundred marks for the out-of-tune thing. Hellwig, whom the club's board still owed a favor, mentally skimmed a hundred marks off the top of this transaction and informed Lützow that the deal was as good as done if he would fork over another fifty marks' commission for him, Hellwig. Handshake.

The next morning had sprung up bright and clear over the craggy volcanic range of Blanche Bay; at one stroke, it had become day, and by six-thirty in the morning it was already as hot as the inside of a German bakery. Eight black men had heaved the piano aboard the little launch that normally ran between the capital and Mioko, and while the remaining clouds from the waning night vaporized in the morning sun, Lützow boarded the ship he had personally rented, sweating out the liqueurs he had been treated to the previous evening, and sailed over to Kabakon with crapulous nerves and a trembling hand on the wobbly moored piano that he intended to present to Engelhardt as a dowry.

Now a series of gay, unburdened days really did begin. Lützow, who always carried a tuning fork with him in his luggage, immediately set himself to the task of liberating the piano—which had been towed by the natives into the library (they had unceremoniously removed a wooden side wall from the house and then simply nailed it back to the house's corner posts)—from the discordant notes that had emanated from it for years. He initiated the instrument's healing process by striking the pure A on his fork and stooping down deep into the innards of the action; he felt about an out-of-tune piano as a painter would a palette lacking the colors red and blue.

Lying naked on the veranda, Engelhardt, who was enjoying his daily sunbath, listened with a smile to the singly struck notes drifting outside and to Lützow, who cheerily whistled all the while. He felt a great and profound respect for artists and their abilities; the fact that he had never been able to muster up either the talent or the discipline to create something like real art provoked a feeling that almost bordered on envy. While squinting his eyes at the horizon, he pondered whether his stay on Kabakon might not indeed be regarded as a work of art. Suddenly the thought occurred to him that possibly he himself was his own artistic artifact and that perhaps the paintings and sculptures exhibited in museums or the performances of famous operas constituted a completely outmoded conception of art—indeed, that only through his, Engelhardt's, existence was the divide between art and life bridged. He smiled again, dispatching this delectable, solipsistic fancy into a secret and remote corner of his edifice of ideas, sat up, and opened a coconut while inspecting the wounds on his legs, which, oozing, had grown ever larger in recent weeks. Dabbing the spots in question first with coconut milk, later with salt water, and then with an iodine tincture, he soon forgot about them.

Engelhardt and Lützow, who quickly developed a heartfelt affinity for each other without mentioning it, explored the isle

together, visited the islanders' villages, and took part as honored guests in all sorts of festivities and dance presentations.
In return, a chief and his children were permitted to visit the
two Germans in their house—for Engelhardt had decided
that Lützow would immediately move into his home and need
not, as the unfortunate Aueckens had, complete a probation-
ary period over in the rattan hut—and, under the watchful
gaze of young Makeli, witness there the piano playing with
which the new arrival delighted those present.

Lützow's slender hands were observed attentively. They
danced back and forth on the cracked ivory keys, managing to
elicit the most glorious cascades of sound from the now exqui-
sitely tuned instrument. The chief insisted on stepping up to
the piano during the performance itself and depressing individual keys with his pinkie (for this finger seemed to him the
most elegant), the sound of which, however, resulted in considerable dissonance within the overall structure of the composi-
tions Lützow had chosen to perform. But it was all the same
to them! Engelhardt and Lützow laughed and were happy
not to be in Rabaul, but among people whose untrained ears
might have been unable to distinguish Liszt from Satie, but
who nevertheless felt music to be something of extraordinary
beauty.

Makeli, whose German skills were making unusual progress (Engelhardt now read every evening from Büchner's *Lenz*,
and after that from Keller's *Green Henry*), reported to them
that over in his village the chief had arranged for a life-sized
piano to be constructed for him from rattan, and in the village
square, under the starry night sky, accompanied by the humming of hundreds of cicadas, he had begun theatrically imitat-

ing Lützow's hand movements on the rattan keyboard (which had been painted in black and white with charcoals and chalk paste) while ardently singing, quite melodiously and almost wholly impromptu.

In those days, however, Makeli also told of a hole in the jungle, a pit twenty feet deep wreathed with sharpened bamboo stakes, at the bottom of which venomous snakes writhed: cobras and the like, vipers, too—even an ancient death adder lived down there in the damp darkness. For generations, the hole had been excavated at a location that was taboo for the tribe to approach. Only the chief and his deputy, as well as a healer who spoke in tongues, were permitted to stand at the edge of the depression and look down inside. Now and again, Makeli said, they would throw a morsel of bristled pig down, very rarely a live dog.

Lützow's numerous sicknesses, meanwhile, were blown away as if by a tropical breeze. His joints neither pained him, nor did he feel that aggressive pressure behind his eyes that had accompanied him for years in Germany and that he, resignedly, had understood as a permanent part of himself. Sniffles and asthmatic attacks no longer cropped up. He was, admittedly, not yet capable of walking around totally naked like his host Engelhardt, but he climbed the trunks of palms at least as nimbly as Makeli to bring down the coconut fruits; breaking them open on stones and separating the shell from the meat with a coconut rasper was enjoyable daily work for him. He fell so in love with the coconut that, shortly after his arrival, he began living off it exclusively.

Engelhardt felt only a minimal speck of envy. Oh, no, he was quite extraordinarily proud of his new arrival, and together they now wrote letters to various vegetarian publications in Germany in which they extolled the nuts: the fruits consumed in the morning, shortly before sunrise, differed so greatly in taste, they wrote, from those broken open in the afternoon that it was as if one were comparing apples and bananas. The nuts of February bore absolutely nothing in common with those picked in April; one might as well compare wheat bran and spinach. They lost themselves in ever more complicated hymns of praise to their sustenance of choice, ending the letters with the suggestion that they now experienced the milk and the meat of the coconuts synesthetically: some nuts reminded them of the festive, mournful sound of Mahler's symphonies, others of the entire blue color spectrum; others, in turn, felt angular on the palate, heart-shaped, or even octagonal.

The relevant newspapers at home published these letters all too gladly. Lützow's descriptions of having established a naked Communist utopia under palm trees while subduing the apparent libertinage with the benevolent morality of the tropical sun's salubrious glow and the incomparably succulent and practical coconut—one ought to visit quickly since one was healed of every disease of civilization in Engelhardt's Order of the Sun—mesmerized certain circles. The *Berliner Illustrirte* even published a caricature under the headline *Der Kokosnußapostel* that showed a very muscular Engelhardt clothed only in a palm frond, a scepter in one hand, in the other an orb in the shape of a coconut, black people dressed in the European manner worshipping at his feet. The famous musician's letters, which first appeared in *Der Naturarzt* and *Vegetarische Warte*, were now reprinted widely, albeit with introductory commentaries that the rather well-known Berlin musician Max Lützow

had gone off the deep end and followed a lunatic into the
South Seas, and hereinafter, if you please, was the epistolary
proof.

After reading this free advertising, quite a few salvation-
seekers started toward German New Guinea: passages on ships
were booked, Engelhardt's booklet *A Carefree Future* was unexpectedly reprinted one, two, and even three times, and various grocers in the Reich were urged to please stock fresh
coconuts. For a brief time, a popular song in which a clever
melody was accompanied by witty lyrics circulated throughout Berlin; children and youngsters sang that ditty about coconuts, man-eaters, and naked Germans in the schoolyards of
the capital until one was no longer safe from the obtrusively
catchy tune—not in streetcars, nor before the opera houses, nor
in the reception halls of the ministries. But the fuss vanished
just as quickly as it had come; the carousel of fads turned too
fast, and *Cocos nucifera* was replaced by excessive consumption
of cocaine; one season later, hot, aerated maize, called *popcorn*,
was all the rage. Meanwhile, visitors were already en route to
the Pacific protectorate and, once docked in Rabaul and spat
out by the respective Imperial Post ship, were standing around
more or less destitute.

Hotel Director Hellwig sent those hoping for cheap ac-
commodation over to the Hotel Deutscher Hof, whose director, an Alsatian who was usually heavily intoxicated by eight
in the morning, in turn sent them back to Hellwig straight-
away, a loaded revolver in his hand. And so the bizarre, half-
naked throng, who hadn't understood at all that Rabaul was
not Kabakon, camped in the meadows of the little town and
on the beach of Blanche Bay. Under sailing tarps they had

hung up between palm trees they slept, covered only in towels, defenseless against the swirling swarms of mosquitoes that lusted after their sweet European blood. Fever pounced on them; after one month, the little clinic was out of quinine powder; in the second, the first visitor died without ever having laid eyes on Kabakon. He was buried next to Heinrich Aueckens, whose plain, unadorned grave no one had made an effort to prettify with fresh flowers. And with every steamship, one or two new unsuspecting souls came and joined the troupe— such that soon nearly two dozen young Germans were living in direst poverty at the edge of the town.

Governor Hahl, now fully healed from the blackwater fever, back in the new capital Rabaul, and worried that a new slum district populated by Germans was forming on his watch, walked with physicians Wind and Hagen down to the new arrivals (the meadows had been given up in favor of a campsite on the beach over which a light sea breeze wafted) to have a serious chat with them. There, in the marsh of sandy sludge at ebb tide, between hermit crabs and mangroves, the doctors and the governor were met with an appalling, almost pagan sight; the heavily emaciated young people loitered listlessly in the shadows of shredded tarps, the ends of which blew back and forth; some were buck-naked; it smelled vaguely of human feces that hadn't been carried completely out to sea by the daily tide; others had fallen asleep, exhausted, while reading anarchist treatises; still others spooned white, slimy meat from halved coconuts into mouths rimmed by unkempt beards.

The representatives of civilization stood among them in light-colored suits. Hahl, who was unable to fend off a certain intellectual sympathy for the young people (on the return voyage from Singapore, along with a French-language volume of Mallarmé's poetry and the scores of several Bach cantatas, he had in fact internalized Engelhardt's *A Carefree Future*), immediately directed the physicians to attend to the worst cases, to have them washed with freshwater and admitted to the little clinic. If beds were no longer available there, they must requisition rooms for the rest of that sad lot in the two hotels, which were mostly empty. And so it happened that Hotel Director Hellwig saw himself unable to refuse Governor Hahl his request to quarter a good dozen of the wastrels in the fastidiously cleaned rooms of the Hotel Fürst Bismarck, cursing himself for not having accommodated those scoundrels two months ago; at least then they would not have been sick and dirty. When afterward the rest of the young people were placed in the rival Hotel Deutscher Hof, its owner fled into his administrative chambers, locked the door from inside, and got so drunk off the contents of a crate of Dutch gin that he was not seen again for three weeks perhaps.

An emissary was dispatched to Engelhardt from the governor's office to Kabakon, carrying the message in a rattan bag that he should report to the capital for a discussion in good time. Since his missionary work had apparently borne overripe fruit, though no one in Rabaul knew what to do with the newly arrived salvation-seekers, the question was whether he might be prepared to defray the expenses his private mythology had incurred, primarily for lodging (all this in Hahl's honestly friendly tone, drafted without a trace of irony). At this, Engelhardt lapsed into a state of lethargy; proclamations from official channels that did not work to his advantage were so crippling that he was no longer capable of action of any kind. He handed the letter to Lützow, who skimmed it and then shouted, Good gracious, but this is all quite splendid—they'd sail over to Rabaul together, pay the hotel bills, and fetch the unfortunate souls over to Kabakon, who had, after all, traveled to the protectorate on his account. They would thus be able to admit several new adepts into the Order of the Sun at one stroke; and wasn't this ultimately his, Engelhardt's, mission—the effective dissemination of his wonderful idea?

Engelhardt scratched himself pensively on one of the now-open wounds on his shin and shoved his thumb in his mouth. Although he had written a multitude of advertising letters and sent them all over the world, he hadn't, to be honest, ever reckoned with the fact that a fair number of unknown persons would actually set out to visit him. Sure, a handful of friends and like-minded people, perhaps, but Hahl had written in his letter of a good twenty-five men and women. Engelhardt was unsure how to deal with them (indeed, they weren't happy black islanders who would let themselves be impressed by something as completely ephemeral as *mana*) and was unsure whether they would accept his authority or whether they would unmask him, reveal him as that which he took himself to be in the secret chambers of his heart, known only to him: a repressed phony. He was certainly glad, though, that Lützow was with him and encouraged him. Alone, he would have simply holed up and ignored the letter and all the consequences that arose from it with his own peculiar cowardice.

After arriving in Rabaul, Engelhardt and Lützow strode down the causeway shaded by palm trees toward the governor's residence. They were of course not walking naked; Engelhardt was wearing the now heavily bleached-out cotton vestment in which he had first arrived in the protectorate, while Lützow had wrapped himself about the hips in a colorful sheet and thrown over his shoulder the now no longer quite clean, collarless formal shirt he had worn during the last of his horrid evening performances at the piano in the German Club.

Engelhardt noticed that nature around the capital had been visibly subdued, that they had driven back the jungle and laid far more decent avenues than they had in Herbertshöhe. What, he thought, could counter this, this revolt of man against the chaos of the organic, this tidying impulse to straighten, this guiding of ectoplasm into well-defined limits? So that was it, the civilizing element, that's what this led to: things moral, boiled, steamed. He needed to cough, faltered, almost falling flat.

On the broad lawn laid out before the governor's residence, a wooden trestle had been erected. They brought a native offender and fastened him to the construction with two crossed rattan straps. Some white-suited planters had turned up, arms folded at the chest, as well as a crowd of jeering children and a delegation of native policemen from the colonial protection force; each policeman had been allotted a tunic and a belt with a bayonet, but neither shoes nor boots, so that in the eyes of the white masters some element of the ridiculous would always cling to his authority. A man from the colonial forces stepped forward, took off his uniform jacket, and—baring a muscular torso with an almost blue-black sheen—received from the white police constable what in his gigantic hands seemed an impossibly delicate and thin bamboo cane. Now the planters were clapping their hands, smirking; the children whistled with their fingers, and while Engelhardt and Lützow turned away, the giant struck the supple cane with unimaginable force against the naked back of the man bound to the trestle.

Lützow gently touched the elbow of his friend, who was wincing on account of the cane strokes, and soon they entered the shadowy retreat of the governor's veranda, on which Hahl stood with legs apart, bobbing up and down, observing the punitive action from a distance, thumbs stuck left and right in his waistband. They all introduced themselves, and the governor seized Engelhardt's hands and shook them quite vigorously. They must follow him inside, please, Hahl said; it seemed as if he were genuinely happy to see them both. In the salon itself it was wondrously cool; Engelhardt counted eight modern electrical fans up there on the ceiling.

That man out there had been a thief, one had to take drastic measures although it didn't suit him at all, he wanted to run the colony differently than, say, his colleagues down in German South-West Africa or in Cameroon, one had to try to incorporate the natives into the principled and impartial German legal system, which was of course a highly moral, fair authority and not, as in the French or Dutch territories, for example (not to mention the Belgian ones), merely a whitewash designed to mask the preservation of a modern form of slavery, which is to say, economic exploitation with maximum profit and minimal humanity.

During these remarks to which the two listened, nodding, justifiably pleased with the governor's almost socialist approach, a Chinese steward brought fruit juices on a silver tray, and a hummingbird with a pale blue gleam, halfheartedly eyeing the juice glasses, strayed into the salon and adeptly navigated between the whirring blades of the ceiling fans only to fly back outside moments later through the open front section of the residence.

Hahl made a quick mental note to make a new file for his card index in which he would theorize about the difficulty of bringing about hovering flight—whether one would perhaps be capable of constructing a flying object that, based on the hummingbird, could hold its position floating in space. The colorful bird, Hahl thought while chatting with these two odd fellows, was really an involuntary perpetuum mobile of nature, so to speak; the hummingbird consumed vast quantities of energy in the form of sweet fructose in order to drink from the calyxes while hovering, which in turn allowed it to feed from them only by so hovering; ergo, if one wanted to build a technical object that could linger in the air, one had to guarantee the energy supply from within, as it were. Well, these were the sorts of amateur scholarly studies that occupied Governor Hahl at the end of his workday.

Now, he had already, in his letter, outlined the reason he had requested they call on the Rabaul residence: quite frankly, it was about the crowd of mostly adolescent visitors whom Engelhardt had lured into the protectorate with his writings. Now, of course—and at this point it must be said, Hahl declared, that he was personally delighted at the pursuit not just of economic and missionary ventures in the colony, but also at running a very interesting philosophical experiment— Engelhardt did not bear any direct liability for the actions of his readers, but all the same, he could not deny a certain moral responsibility, especially in view of their health. One unfortunate man had already passed away from the fever (at the moment

Hahl uttered this, a morphic phantom pain stirred in him, his body momentarily recalling at subatomic levels the destructive power of malaria it had recently experienced), and thus they had taken the throng of completely ignorant and unprepared new arrivals from the outdoor camp they had chosen for themselves— teeming with pathogens and just bristling with filth—and placed them in the little infirmary and the local hotels.

From Engelhardt's ear, meanwhile, came warm drops, then, trickling down, a small hot rivulet. He turned his head to the side to see what was running onto his shoulder so unexpectedly. His garb was suddenly stained yellow by a load of earwax that had dissolved into a flow. What an astounding, uncontrollable, childlike amount. He repressed the urge to plunge his finger into his ear and usher the secretion to his mouth for a taste, but instead sat somewhat sideways so that Hahl and Lützow could not see the stains, raised his glass with the fruit juice, acted as if he were such a spellbound listener that he missed his slightly open mouth with the glass, and deftly spilled a few splotches of juice onto his shoulder such that the ear discharge was not only unrecognizable, but also completely covered by the like-colored drink.

Now Hahl had just mentioned the writings of the French thinker Charles Fourier in some detail (the sound of the final lashes on the back of the alleged thief outside had faded in the square) and handed Engelhardt a napkin, with which he wiped off his shoulder in theatrical exaggeration, whereupon Lützow, who hadn't read Fourier, but had read a little of Proudhon (one of his erstwhile girlfriends had been a bomb maker in Dublin), remarked that the Order of the Sun was indeed a place of social renewal and it was just splendid that the governor not only tolerated it, but supported it morally and intellectually, so to speak, because they had, well, begging his pardon, always assumed that a supreme state authority like Hahl here was a natural foe of individual utopia. Freedom was first and foremost freedom from property; that's how they lived on Kabakon, and that's how they would keep on living.

Engelhardt, who not only found Lützow's sudden amateur foray into political matters disturbing, but who was also inwardly astonished that the man was now styling himself a theoretician of his, Engelhardt's, ideological constructs, interjected that Fourier had been a notorious anti-Semite, that Engelhardt had purchased Kabakon lawfully and was by no means professing anarchism, and that what Fourier had imagined as *phalanstère* (Engelhardt was absolutely certain that Lützow didn't know the term) was an expression of a shabby, Philistine utopia of the petit bourgeois governed, to top it all off, by an obsessive sex drive.

Lützow looked at his friend and immediately went silent. The governor, taking note of this little skirmish within the cocovore brothers' power structure in his mind's file cabinet, clapped his hands and said that it was, to be sure, extremely edifying to have conversations like this in such a godforsaken place, but one now had to return to reality, if the gentlemen would allow it; this week, he still had to look after a cholera outbreak in Kavieng, and, at the end of the month, a proper tribal feud (with casualties) on Astrolabe Bay, then the famous American author Jack London had planned a visit, and now could they put their minds together, please, and address what should happen to the young adepts who had been lured to Rabaul by the call of the Order of the Sun.

So they walked over together to the Hotel Fürst Bismarck, fetched the physician Wind on the way, and had an indignant Director Hellwig, who was now no longer quite so amicably disposed toward Engelhardt, show them the throngs of new-comers napping away either their afternoon or their convales-cence. Hahl folded his arms over his broad chest as if he did not wish to comment on the whole affair for the time being. Dr. Wind turned out to be fairly hostile toward cocovorism. He bent over the patients dozing on the hotel beds that had been pushed out into the corridors, raised an eyelid here and there, and commented at a whisper how truly damaging it was for the human person to live exclusively from one nutrient. Yes, those wounds, for example, there on Mr. Engelhardt's legs, which were now covered in pus, would not only be unable to heal cleanly and properly because of the tropically induced damp, but in fact were precisely the result of pronounced mal-nutrition. Begging pardon, but that was nonsense, Lützow re-plied in a loud voice, for it was evident to everyone that in his case those very innumerable ailments he had been unable to fend off in Germany for years had vanished, all of them, com-pletely, on account of the coconut diet he had adopted here.

When talk came around to coconuts, here and there the young people in the beds began to stir: waking from their light sleep, they suddenly saw August Engelhardt in their midst and in the flesh, the same gaunt figure they had seen illustrated in various newspapers at home and because of whom they had set out. A murmuring of recognition went through the hallways, a Swabian boy, barely of age, called out with a croak, *Savior!*, a young woman rose from her sickbed, walked shakily toward Engelhardt, knelt down, seized his hand, and under the bewildered gazes of the visitors finally sank floorward to caress the feet of Engelhardt. who looked extremely embarrassed.

Wind and Lützow lifted the girl up off the floor, mumbling, *Come, come,* and Hahl, unable to suppress an amused smile at the absurdity of the scene, conducted Engelhardt with a firm hand back toward the hotel lobby, where the latter was informed by Director Hellwig point-blank that he had to bear the costs these deranged people had incurred, immediately and without ceremony. Engelhardt retreated deeply into himself, sucking his thumb. Governor Hahl formed a cathedral with his fingertips under his nose and said, *Slowly now, please.* Mustn't it lie within the realm of possibility to reallocate certain debts Engelhardt owed to Queen Emma in such a way that his plantation's copra production could be borrowed against in this case, too? Exactly, very good, he would sign everything, our friend yammered, indeed he was prepared to do anything, just send these horrible people back, he wanted nothing to do with them, they all ought to be transported back to Germany, at his expense. Indeed, that was likely the most prudent course, the governor replied, quickly calculating that passage on a ship for around twenty-five individuals would nevertheless add up to a grand total of twelve thousand five hundred marks.

They agreed: to send the confused young people back, that Engelhardt, in order to defray these costs, would borrow against his own production for several more years, and finally that future visitors to the Order of the Sun would only be let aboard in Germany by Norddeutscher Lloyd if they could prove that they had sufficient funds to transport themselves from the protectorate back to the Reich. Engelhardt for his part would pledge to send no further letters of advertisement with proclamations that New Pomerania was the alleged Garden of Eden. In fact, it was best if he wrote no further letters of any kind. There was a crackling and rushing in Engelhardt's ear as if he were standing underwater, as if an ocean were engulfing him. He shoved his thumb in his mouth once more. Lützow stood somewhat off to the side during this horse trade and nibbled with irritation on a cuticle.

Later, Governor Hahl was himself standing under water, lathering up listlessly under the tepidly drizzling shower he had had installed in his new bathroom after the relocation of the capital, because he preferred being sprinkled from above to lying moronically in the tub. After the two oddballs had trotted off, he had opened the letter with the official seal that he had been carrying around with him for some time in expectation of good news (the document came from the new Berlin office of his friend Wilhelm Solf, who had just been named director of the Imperial Colonial Office), but in its stead he had to endure an incendiary three-page screed: what in the hell was going on there under his aegis; indeed, whenever the German press reported on New Guinea, it only ever mentioned that the protectorate was evidently in a state of libertinage, populated by naked Germans who engaged in orgies, who subsisted on flowers and butterflies; if he wished to retain his well-remunerated post (and Solf was saying this as a friend) and did not want to find himself occupying a pathetic clerical office in the subterranean bowels of the Berlin Imperial Colonial building, then he must see to it forthwith that these undisciplined conditions cease immediately (Solf was sparing himself the mitigating word *please*). Only a few drops more found their way out of the showerhead onto the governor's scalp, which he had scrubbed to a froth with a fragrant and yet slightly caustic hair soap. Then the water ran out, and Hahl stood half blind and dripping in the gubernatorial shower; stifling the onset of an outburst of rage, he pondered what exactly should be done now.

Come evening, Engelhardt and Lützow sailed back to Kabakon; under a fading orange-red sky, they said nothing to each other, though not as if they were among friends and therefore needn't talk for a few hours, but in the awareness that something had shattered and couldn't be pieced back together. A few times, Lützow attempted to break the spell and make his friend smile with a poetic interjection regarding the enchanted cascades of clouds, but Engelhardt was having none of it; in fact, he heard every seemingly casual remark about the course of their visit in Rabaul as pedantic, enervating counsel directed at him.

After reaching the isle, he even forbade his friend from sitting down at the piano, withdrew to his bed, and—the sonorous snoring of the virtuoso had just begun filling their shared home—stared up at the ceiling for many hours, sucking his thumb, without thinking about anything at all, until he got bogged down again so deeply in a specific thought that the latter cast itself over the entire essence of the world and over the all-expansive, infinitely vast cosmos like a flaming *mene mene* (or perhaps like an ouroboros, that mythological serpent gorging on its own tail).

Again he saw that wheel of fire that his mother had shown him when he was a little boy. And when it appeared above him on the ceiling of the house, rotating on its own axis, and since he had no pillow with which to cover his eyes, he buried his face in his hands, groaning in terror. Animals then appeared to him, tremendous creatures akin to the *genius malignus*, their sight so unspeakably gruesome that he curled up into a ball in horror, miserably seeking shelter in the darkest recesses of his own person. Beasts whose dreadful names he was afraid to utter, hideous beings that were called *Hastur* and *Azathoth* and whispered to him, hissing, that mankind was an insignificant, irrelevant, completely negligible bagatelle in the universe whose fate it was to appear and pass away again unnoticed and unlamented. Lützow, who wouldn't have understood such things at all, slept, slept, did not even stir when Engelhardt stooped over him just before dawn, wondering how he could kill him without waking him up.

Part Three

X

While Captain Christian Slütter is slogging through the last, still furiously seething tails of a July storm that incessantly sends breakers from the Solomon Sea crashing over the deck of his rusty boil–covered freighter, the SS *Jeddah*, Max Lützow is boarding, bright and early, the same little launch on which he arrived in Kabakon almost a year ago. Both vessels are steaming inevitably toward each other. The center of the cyclone, meanwhile, has rolled by two hundred nautical miles north. Over in Apia, Slütter has dropped two hundred crates of French brandy that he had taken aboard in Sydney in adverse circumstances, and he is now ferrying kitchen appliances, knives, axes, pans, and such up to New Pomerania.

Lützow, by contrast, had packed his bag one morning before sunrise, gently touched the piano in passing with the tips of his fingers, and before Engelhardt awoke, walked down to the beach to be rowed out to the launch awaiting him beyond the lagoon by Makeli, who was smiling inscrutably to himself.

The secret departure was preceded by a terrible argument

the prior evening. Engelhardt had been convinced his comrade had stolen the scissors he himself had in fact inadvertently misplaced. During a downpour that drummed on the roof, as the mosquitoes became such a nuisance that both had coated themselves in a thick layer of coconut oil and lit several coir fires, and when a certain hopelessness in the situation became apparent, Engelhardt had swept the white chess figures off the board with a surly wipe of the hand. Knight and rook had landed, like wooden grenades, in the sand beside a millipede, which, sorely disturbed in its consumption of the leaf that was its supper, crept off sullenly in the rain. Engelhardt had brought up the missing scissors again, and Lützow, who despite all his shortcomings had no intention of arguing purely for the sake of argument, replied that he had no knowledge of any scissors, and the matter didn't interest him anyway—weren't all items communal property, including the scissors in question? He was quite prepared, Lützow said, to overlook this little tropical hysteria, but he was not about to take farfetched, unjustified accusations sitting down. *Unjustified accusations*, Engelhardt blurted out—leaping to his feet, running back into the house, and beginning, in a kind of frenzy, to pull individual volumes from the bookshelves and throw them out the open window into the rain—they most certainly were not, no, several times now Lützow had fancied himself a secret theoretician of his order, though in truth he, Engelhardt, had invented and planned everything, such that he now had to ask himself when the musician would finally take over control of Kabakon, it was only a question of time, after all, but he intended to put a stop to this as quickly as possible because this island, contrary to the remarks Lützow had made to Hahl, was in no way a democracy, and least of all some infantile Communist collective, nor would it ever be. Engelhardt alone determined where it was going, and Lützow's advice to settle that horde of nutcases from Rabaul on Kabakon had essentially been a malicious attempt at a coup, which had only served to deprive him of power in the long run.

Fine, Lützow replied, then he would just leave if so little value was placed on his presence; he had thought, perhaps in error, that they were together on Kabakon to establish a new Eden. And he, who was by nature an altogether affable fellow, was in no way scheming to take anything away from Engelhardt, and least of all was he thinking of making demands for power, which would get him absolutely nothing on a coconut plantation, because he was an artist and not an accountant— in short, he was really very sorry if he had given some other impression, but now he needed to—he wanted to—go, and he wished his friend good luck. He was truly sad; after all, he had felt an intimacy between them, for the disintegration of which he probably had himself partly to blame (*That's right, that's right*, Engelhardt said, nodding grimly), but regardless of how it was about to end, his friend had taught and shown him a lot, that there was a way to escape the stupefying plight of modern existence, and for that he would always be thankful. The scissors, incidentally, would reappear a few days later as if they had never been missing.

One faded photograph of the two still exists showing them with full beards in front of a palm tree; Lützow, half supine, bemused, his left arm braced against the sand, is looking straight at the camera; Engelhardt, startlingly scrawny, shows his crow-like profile. It's an oddly strained, haughty way to hold one's head, which could perhaps be confused with pretension; but it also expresses self-confidence, even a hint of smugness. By now his belly stretches over the checkered waistcloth, distended, globular, undernourished; he is far beyond sucking it in out of vanity before the shutter mechanism of the camera is depressed with a click.

Alas, so Lützow turned out to be a decent enough person—he had doubtless always been one, a little vain perhaps, but certainly had not allowed the touches of twisted, malevolent misanthropy that Engelhardt had been displaying for some time (the ghoulish intentions he harbors regarding Lützow and others shall remain hidden in a shadowy side corridor of his psyche for a while yet) to provoke him. Lützow acted most fairly toward his friend, and so his morning exodus from Kabakon, though it doesn't quite seem like it to him, is in fact a respectable course of action and not some slithering away.

The natives already working in the plantation this early morning observe him sailing away and view his departure, whispering with one another, as a bad omen on which even worse will follow. Indeed, yesterday they had seen a peculiar, unknown bird pitifully wallowing in the sand as if it wanted to get rid of something gumming up its plumage. A collective decision is made to lay down their work and do nothing but wait for more signs to manifest themselves. That Engelhardt hasn't been paying his employees for almost two years now isn't seen as particularly grave, since they assume their employer simply has no money at his disposal right now. The Tolai chief, who so enthusiastically played on the rattan piano by night, having now thoroughly outgrown what seem to him as the primitive drums and whistles of his race, is sitting somewhat off to the side under a palm tree and rubbing his numb hands, feeling a deep sadness at the departure of the white music conjurer that is infinitely increased by the fact, conscientiously concealed from his tribe, that he has contracted leprosy.

Engelhardt—and neither he nor Max Lützow knows this—has likewise caught leprosy, and this disease, whose Old Testament nimbus obscures the simple reality that it is primarily a nervous disorder, causes certain addled reactions within Engelhardt's person, which is already deranged from several years of his unhealthy diet. Dr. Wind, over in the Rabaul area, was of course quite right in his own way.

Now, it would probably be overstating things to say that Engelhardt's psyche had drunk from the river Lethe, on whose shores it had long been resting, gazing at its own reflection, sinking into the most profound cosmic forgetfulness about why he had ever come here in the first place. The truth looks much more mundane; the farther he removes himself from the community of man, the more outlandish his behavior and relationship to it grows. He is thrown back into an atavistic mental state that expresses itself in a premonition of total loss of control: the bottles with Kabakon Oil piling up in Rabaul are consigned to oblivion, copra production has halted, the pages of his beloved books curl in the tropical humidity because they are no longer regularly set out to air in the sunshine, yes, even the flowers around his house, which he had tended before with nurturing love, have become overgrown and are in danger of being strangled by creepers. Yes, it is as if he has become the old spinster Miss Havisham, who stolidly awaits that great, all-consuming conflagration that might finally deliver her.

And what of the leprosy? The ostensible epicenter of infection lay somewhere within the perfect fifth formed by the C and G keys on Lützow's piano, where a scab loosened from the Tolai chief's leprous finger remained, which Engelhardt a short time later took for his own and, as a matter of routine and reflex, stuck in his mouth without bearing in mind or imagining that there were several bleeding spots in his oral cavity and on the gums, so-called canker sores. In truth, our friend had been infected years before, of course.

XI

So while Engelhardt persists in furious, paralyzed, in-
flamed derangement on Kabakon (a neurologist would
have diagnosed severe paranoia) and Max Lützow, a
genuine lump in his throat, chugs toward Rabaul feeling cheerful and relieved in spite of everything, Captain Christian Slütter, standing on the bridge of the *Jeddah* (which essentially
consists of a crooked steel structure open astern), rounds a spit
of land jutting bottle-green into Blanche Bay and sights first the
smoking cone of the volcano and then the little German town
spreading out so tidily before him. He recalls with a smile
his last stay, when he still did not possess a captain's license,
and—running his hand through the blond beard (which is already showing several white hairs, which before, during the visit
a few years back, were present only subcutaneously)—moves the
crank of the chadburn up to half ahead. Stuck in the inside
pocket of Slütter's white, dirty, always half-wet captain's jacket is
a letter received in Apia from Governor Hahl, and in it the request to report to the new capital Rabaul for a discussion about
eliminating a small but pressing problem.

The blustering has been replaced by a glassy, picture-book sea, the sun appears, he sticks a moist cigarette between his lips and hums a little melody known only to him. Looking at the whole scene stretched out before him, and himself in it, he is reminded of perusing decades-old albums and the gradually fading photographs in them. It's as if one had seen it this way once before, exactly like this, only now the outer world and oneself have changed, while the album has not—it still radiates intensely out of the past, which in reality lasts forever, while the present, by contrast, consumes itself in fractions of a second. Slütter draws on his cigarette and is forced to laugh because his brain absolutely cannot wrap itself around these paradoxical lines of thought. If you snatch at it, the thought goes poof; if you ambush it, it fades at the moment of insight. Only his own death, he thinks, is predestined; even now this event is inscribed in the future, he only lacks its coordinates, its precise calibration in space and time.

On the freighter, besides Apirana, a Maori with imposing facial tattoos he hired in New Caledonia as an experienced seaman, and Mr. November, the stoker, there's also the young girl Pandora. Slütter picked her up in Sydney; she more or less bumped into him after he'd slept off his opium dreams, smoking as he does twice yearly in Sydney's Chinatown, and had staggered back down to his freighter that afternoon. He'd turned the corner to the quay on Darling Harbour, slightly off-kilter; there, between magnificent barques and whitewashed liners, had lain the *Jeddah*, that ugly, beloved freighter of indeterminate color, peppered in barnacles. And as soon as he had sized up her quarterdeck and the already smoking funnel, bleary-eyed, and tossed his kit bag to a coolie, there was Pandora standing before him, barefoot, red-haired, maybe twelve, maybe fourteen, a little eyebrow raised deftly, a bag slung over her slender shoulder with several pencils and a Hawaiian quilt in it.

With an almost imperceptible nod, she had indicated the four policemen approaching from some distance down the quay and more emphatically than piteously begged him, please, to hide her or take her aboard his ship, it being at any rate imperative that she hide from the menacingly approaching constables. Slütter hadn't hesitated for a moment and took her, past the indifferent looks of the Maori, belowdecks into the captain's cabin of the *Jeddah*, put a blanket over her and his index finger to his lips, then went to the bridge, gave the order to put to sea, and ordered Mr. November to hoist the Imperial merchant flag astern, whereupon the *Jeddah*, belying her battered exterior, had quite spiritedly and briskly made her way from Sydney Harbour out into the open sea.

Pandora sleeps in the cabin for a long time; she sleeps until the coast of New South Wales has long since disappeared from the horizon and the ocean under the *Jeddah* has taken on an inky blue color, and when she awakens and toddles on deck, brushes the bright red, uncombed hair out of her face right and left, and Slütter abandons the helm, she goes and stands beside him and tenderly leans her slender head against the tails of his dirty white captain's jacket. It is then that Slütter knows he will never demand an explanation for why she has fled aboard his ship or ask her who she is.

The sea is forgiving; at the thought of the ocean, some imagine murder, but he feels an infinitely tender, nostalgically tinged affection for a time when Earth was still devoid of people. In this he is perhaps not unlike Engelhardt, but his ideas and dreams never show him a world other than our own, he sees no future race spreading out and no new order arising, but only and always: the sea that with blood-warm, organic imperturbability inundates churches, cities, countries, whole continents.

Is Slütter perhaps deeply in love with Pandora? Or does he see himself too clearly in the role of fatherly protector to allow himself to appreciate Pandora as a young woman whenever she slinks across the upper deck in the afternoon like a disinterested, ginger-colored cat? In any case, he intends to drop her off in German Samoa, but nothing will come of that because when the *Jeddah* sails into Apia Bay and she sees the Union Jack hoisted on the roof of a trading post, she throws herself down before him screaming and crying and bludgeoning the iron deck with her tiny fists so fiercely that her hands tear open on the sides, bleeding, all the while secretly squinting upward with her pretty eyes to see whether her disgraceful antics are laid on too thick. But Slütter's heart is soft like caoutchouc, and he instructs November and Apirana to have the cognac crates unloaded. He takes aboard the pans (and some crates of crabmeat in tins) and comforts the girl by stroking her hair and telling her she may remain on the *Jeddah* up until New Pomerania.

The Maori bandages Pandora's hands, November (whose clothes and skin are covered with layers of ever-darkening soot) loads coal, and a short time later—they are back on the high seas—the storm appears before them, slate-gray, forbidding, and with the intensity of an enormous beast. Mountains of clouds swell up within minutes, their interior illuminated whitish yellow by the convulsive fireworks of a thunderstorm.

The compass needle on the bridge begins whirring around anarchically in the glass circle; towering breakers propel the freighter forward as if it were merely made of cardboard; from the top of a crest, it rushes down into the next wave trough and then back up again such that even Apirana gets queasy. As if he were a reborn real-life Queequeg, the Maori ties himself with a rope to the bulwark nearest the bridge in order to shout the correct course to Slütter with all his might, a course which he foresees more precisely than a compass ever could—he has his ancestors' secret affinity for navigation and seafaring. To both, however, it increasingly seems as if the *Jeddah* is about to capsize at any moment. Slütter feels tears of fury well up in him that taste like iron.

But Mr. November is working like a demon down in the darkness of the hull; scoop by steady scoop of coal lands in the orange-glowing furnace under the boiler. From time to time he tosses the spade aside and yanks at the regulators and valves of the infernal machineries, only then to immediately resume shoveling; this goes on hour after hour. Fire is his métier; it is not just a battle against the hurricane that November is fighting there in the engine room, but an almost primeval struggle against nature itself; it is the ancient insurrection of a demiurge who, in defiance of the elemental chaos, raises the iron shovel one hundred thousand times against the impertinence of cosmic disorder.

Pandora, who has never undertaken such a voyage, sits cowering and shivering with fear in one corner of Slütter's cabin. Every time another bottle shatters or an instrument hurtles toward the opposite wall, she howls in the certainty that the last hour of her short life has come. She senses how the monstrous sea threatens to dash the freighter to pieces; it is the notion of the immense amount of water outside that causes her mortal fear, those mile-deep abysses beneath her, the thought of the eyeless, tasseled, slimy creatures down below in the eternal murk. And Slütter, who cannot leave the bridge under any circumstances, sends Apirana in his place down to the cabin; he is to hold her tight in his arms and caress her head while singing a gentle Maori song.

The storm lasts two days and three nights, in the course of which Apirana, November, and Slütter imbibe jet-black, sugared coffee by the quart, though otherwise take no food, and when the weather finally breaks, it is as if a high fever were departing an oppressed body; an oblique column of light rams through the ashen cloud front, the world sighs with relief, the sea becalms itself, and exhausted frigate birds alight on the abused forecastle of the *Jeddah*. Stray breakers still spray up the sides of the hull, but praise God it's over. Pandora clambers out of the cabin on deck and sits down on a tightly frapped crate of tins, drawing up her bare legs without a word of greeting but aware of having emerged victorious from an epic trial by fire, letting her hair blow in the salty wind.

Her tears are not held against her; even Mr. November, who has ascended from the depths of the freighter and is washing the soot from his face and hands in a bucket dropped into the sea, forces a fleeting, laconic smile as he passes by her; no glue binds people together as tightly as mortal danger jointly endured. And in the brief moment his face lights up, one can manage to guess at the real November, a sensitive, handsome, somber man trying to conceal some long-past sadness from himself forever.

Slütter examines the cargo; nothing has been washed into the ocean except a small crate of frying pans. It is unclear to him why Australian tins of crabmeat have been ordered in the protectorate when the most delectable crabs can be had fresh from the ocean. He shrugs, smokes a cigarette, and steers the *Jeddah* unswervingly northwest. Around one o'clock in the afternoon he sights another ship, the *Karaboudjian*. It is also a freighter, but on a southerly course, toward Darwin. He radios with the Marconi device, but there is no reply, and he calls Pandora to see if she might open a few cans and heat up the contents for them. Soon the *Jeddah* is trailing invisible, alluringly aromatic billows of scent behind it.

While they eat together, Apirana offers to tattoo the girl, to inscribe her skin forever with the history of the storm they've sailed through, but Slütter will have none of this and forbids it, unable to bear seeing her outer shell, her pale epidermis, pierced with needles. The Maori shrugs; it means nothing to him, aside from the knowledge that this part of the chronicle of the course of the world, to which every person is entitled, will not be readable on the young girl. And he descends into the engine room to bring November a plate of steaming crabmeat.

It is a curious love that binds these two. Pandora has unconditionally selected Slütter as master of her fate, and he seems to have gained a certain single-mindedness through her that he did not think himself capable of. He suddenly feels himself to be, to the extent this is even possible, a more profound person; he now no longer views the sea as an extinguishing, all-purifying element, but rather is beginning to comprehend Pandora's fear of its depths. He understands why he as an individual may be a part of everything, but is still, in the totality of things, more negligible than a little chunk of coral that over millions of years is ground into ephemeral sand on the utmost periphery of cosmic perception. In these moments, Slütter takes a wary step closer to death.

And finally, almost like a dog beaten and crippled that furtively slinks off under a bridge to let its wounds heal, the *Jeddah* sails into Blanche Bay. No one is waiting on the quay for its arrival, waving. No one hurries to welcome the battered boat into Rabaul's harbor. Standing on the bridge, Slütter gives instructions regarding the anchor and the moorings, which are carried out halfheartedly by Apirana and Mr. November, while Pandora, after ascertaining that no British police detachment is waiting for her, leaps off onto the wooden landing pier in a bright dress and runs barefoot, past the bobbing launches, straight toward the governor's residence, whose whitewashed façade she espied while they were still entering the bay. Halfway there, she stoops to pick flowers, and a few islander children join her shyly. From a distance, it looks as if they are playing together; Pandora forgets why she has come ashore.

November likewise disembarks to find a representative of the trading post that ordered the cargo on the *Jeddah*. The visit to Rabaul after the storm has something quite anticlimactic about it, and it is all the same to Slütter if someone takes an interest in the frying pans or not. He watches Pandora from over there and knows that he will lose her again—never before has something been important to him, no one has ever had power over him; indeed, he thinks, he himself allowed that red-haired child to make him not only vulnerable but mortal.

He idly buttons up his captain's jacket and grabs his cap to walk over to the governor's residence. He has banished to the farthest reaches of his consciousness his mistrust of authority because he has heard that Hahl, the local governor, is a very decent, levelheaded man. Nevertheless, he cannot shake the feeling that his fate will now increasingly be influenced by others; everything is slipping from his grasp, as in a game of chess, the unavoidable loss of which becomes exponentially more apparent after the third or fourth move—just the other way around, of course, as if it were possible to divine the form of the old tree already present within the seed. He smiles en passant at Pandora, who has sat down on the lawn with the native children, and when she doesn't smile back, indeed, when she doesn't even look up at him, he closes his eyes and keeps going.

The prevailing view that time is an inexorable stream in which everything has its precise beginning and its clearly defined course has also grown entrenched in Slütter's thinking; and yet, as is made plain to him in many a lucid moment, it's more that the end is in fact certain—not the perennial present that will lead us there. The perfidious, inconceivable *now* meanders like an ectoplasmic swirl, out of every nook and cranny, and flows uncontrollably, like a gas, into every direction of existence, disregarding the irrevocable uniqueness of every one of its moments, including the following one:

Captain Slütter punctually presents himself for his appointment with the governor, declines the glass of beer offered with two slightly raised hands, and sits down gingerly as if he suspects that something crucial, something thoroughly unpleasant, will follow. Hahl clears his throat and asks if he might get right to the point, please. He knows, of course, that Slütter is no wayward beachcomber, one of those white reprobates who people the Pacific and live from hand to mouth. But there are certain circumstances that necessitate measures that must be taken, so to speak, outside the law. And someone like Slütter (Hahl stands up abruptly while saying this), who lives betwixt and between, has no family (he couldn't, of course, Slütter thinks, know anything about Pandora), cruises around back and forth for years in the Pacific Ocean owing to his love of freedom, which Hahl respects greatly, by the way, but which prevents the captain from feeling at home anywhere longer than necessary—someone like him must handle a trifle for Hahl, please, one which may not be morally irreproachable, but which is utterly essential.

To wit: August Engelhardt, whom Slütter met several years ago in the old capital Herbertshöhe, has become somewhat of a liability; there have been deliberations for some time, he is heavily in debt now, his island doesn't belong to him at all, the plantation is overgrown, it's quite clear that he's gone insane, Hahl has looked upon the whole matter rather indulgently for years, but now, to make it quick and easy (he is kneading his hands behind his back the whole time), he would ask Slütter, since Hahl is responsible as the ultimate legal authority here, to sail over to Kabakon, shoot the coconut apostle dead, burn his corpse, and scatter the ashes into the sea. He is offering him two thousand marks to do this, from a secret war chest for which he is solely responsible. There is no evidence of it and no obligation to balance accounts, Slütter need neither confirm receipt of the money nor pay any fiscal courtesy calls to the German Reich. Hahl merely requires a willing man who can fire one or two shots and afterward leave the protectorate.

Slütter has to cough and looks at his hands. Silence. No, he will not do it. That, he says, is a guilt he does not want to live with. Hahl, who lights a cigarette and, suggesting pensiveness, watches the smoke from the burning orange tip curl quietly upward for a while, begins his disquisition, yes, he can see that the feeling of guilt has had its source in the civilizing of the man who, under pressure to live in an organized society, directs his aggressive instinct inward, ergo against himself. Engelhardt presumably thinks similarly. But nonetheless and in the end: this is a colony. And the concept of a colony comprises the terms *planting, processing, settling, developing, making profitable*, indeed, *making useful*. Those are the systems with which he is working. His office, which assigns him, above all, to represent the interests of the German people, empowers him to exercise legal, reasonable force to sustain the colony. If his ambit is touched, as in this case, by anarchy and lunacy, however, then he must act, even take extreme measures; that is, so to speak, his categorical imperative (that everything over on Kabakon is now far worse than he describes lies beyond the faculties of his imagination).

Slütter, who does not read philosophers, says no a second time, takes his captain's hat, and rises to leave. Does he at least own a revolver? Hahl wants to know. Yes, quite, down on the *Jeddah* he keeps one. And Hahl, who would not occupy his post if he could not act with an expediency bordering on cruelty, offers the seaman a brief farewell with a nod, the latter having already stepped out onto the veranda, at which point the governor conjures from his jacket pocket a letter from which it emerges that the young girl Pandora, only daughter of Frederic Thesiger, Viscount Chelmsford, governor of New South Wales, who has fled from a boarding school in Sydney, is to be detained in Rabaul until the pertinent representatives of His Britannic Majesty George have arrived here, collected her, and conveyed her back to Australia. Slütter winces, imperceptibly, sleepwalks back into the parlor, sits down again, shakes his head, surrenders; it is enough. Hahl, who holds out the letter to him and goes over to the sideboard to pour them both a glass of whiskey, has won.

XII

In the evening, Lützow sits somewhat off to the side on the grassy knoll next to the governor's residence. Chains of pretty Chinese lanterns are hanging between the tops of the palms, fireflies are rising from the bushes, dancing. A swarm of thousands upon thousands of bats flies soundlessly inland to spend the night sleeping deep in the jungle. The sun has already set, but off behind the volcano, the distant glow of gently fading day can still be discerned. Captain Slütter, wearing his white uniform, sits on the veranda smoking, lost in thought; his cruel mission overwhelms him. Beside him, Pandora, whose feet rest in dainty patent-leather shoes (where on earth did she get them?) and don't quite reach the floor, is devouring a large plate of ginger cookies. On the lawn, the good Dr. Wind sings "Che gelida manina" from *La Bohème* to an amused semicircle of planters. Hahl is for some reason not present; liveried Chinese pass around glasses with sugary punch, and Lützow smokes his first cigarette in a year, which tastes fantastic, a German brand. With his fingertip, he removes a speck of tobacco from his lower lip and is looking out onto the darkening bay when a woman of a certain age saunters up to him and with casual elegance declares without introducing herself that while she is relieved Lützow is now no longer over with that naked man, it seems he needed that time away, he looks to have regained his health, the health of his soul.

Lützow, whose recollections of what had then seemed to him horrific musical performances in the German Club have faded and are now not only coated in the veneer of many months on Kabakon, but in fact have passed completely out of his mind due to the confusing relocation of the capital to Rabaul, turns to Queen Emma and gazes at a dark, pleasant, open face whose mouth, slightly agape, reveals two immaculate rows of teeth, which in turn are separated by the barely visible tip of her tongue. He is struck as if by an electric shock. With his slender hands he clasps her waist, draws her close to him in a rather manly way, and kisses her with dark red, ecstatic abandon.

Meanwhile, Engelhardt, under cover of incipient darkness over on Kabakon, has begun excavating twenty-foot-deep holes with his axe (some on the beach, others deep in the jungle), to an obscure purpose known only to himself. He covers these over with branches and palm fronds as soon as the exhausting work is completed, as if he plans to blanket the island with mantraps. Lützow leads Emma down to the deserted beach coated by the pallid light of the now-risen full moon. Soon they sink to the ground, and the aura of their suppleness falters, movements become automated, which, when observed from a distance, approximate the rhythm of an absurd man-machine; they seem like half-naked mannequins, pursuing a spastic dance while lying intertwined on the ground. The moon shines on

the two bouncing orbs of Lützow's blond-haired buttocks raised
aloft; now and again the sound of moaning drifts over toward
the governor's residence, even though there is no wind. A few
nautical miles northward, a naked, limping Engelhardt roams
through the jungle of his island under the same full moon,
the axe in his raised hands.

The following day, Lützow and Emma decide not only to
leave Rabaul together, but also to get married as quickly as
possible. A few suitcases are hurriedly packed, the double doors
to Villa Gunantambu bolted with a large padlock, and while
the members of the German Club (with the women leading the
way) meet for a kind of spontaneous, extraordinary plenary as-
sembly, the sole aim of which is to heap as much ridicule as
possible upon Queen Emma and her musician, to blanket both
with the filth of their malevolent *ressentiments*, the pair walk
over to the governor's residence, followed by a throng of black
porters, to ask Hahl to marry them then and there. Emma is
wearing her much-used wedding gown, which hasn't been a
pristine white for years now.

Hahl, who has been quite unhappily in love with Emma for
over a decade, though no one would remotely suspect it, has
of course already heard about the affair. From time to time, it
seems to him as if reality, as tenuous as it already is, is slipping
away from him: such is the case now as the two stand before
him smiling dreamily, and he, a short time ago still permitting
himself pangs of conscience about having ordered a murder,
which was perhaps dreadfully cowardly after all, summons to
his face a diplomatic, if not to say fake smile, conveys his best
wishes to both, and asks Lützow with a wink if he has indeed
thought this over well. Lützow, as if he could already see the

immediate future, declaims with a handsome grin: *Yet drunken the singer, not heeding the warning, back into the maelstrom turns now his gaze.*

A tie is located quickly; laughing, Hahl lends one of his, yes, in this he is unprincipled and bighearted, especially as he is so happy that Lützow has evidently landed back in civilization again; no, no, he does not intend to marry them—an excuse is found just as fast as the tie is lent—he cannot find his pince-nez, they ought to go on without him, the youngsters (Emma is long past fifty), Slütter is a captain, after all, he, too, has the right to officiate, shoo, down to the jetty on the shore, he will follow presently, then he'll down a glass of spumante to their health, better yet two or three, haha. And Hahl, who has seen Emma marry all too often already, of course does not follow, but observes them both as they coo their way down to the *Jeddah*, dolefully opens the door to his study (there, behind glass, in a mahogany frame, hangs the ubiquitous reproduction of Böcklin's *Isle of the Dead*), slams the door behind him with a crash, sits down behind the desk, buries his gubernatorial face in those manly, suntanned paws, and weeps with a lack of restraint that surprises him most of all.

Down on the quay, euphoric, the two ask Captain Slütter to marry them aboard the *Jeddah*. He clears his throat, scratches at his chin, shifts his weight from one leg to another, coughs, and then does agree after all, although he—this, please, they ought to note—has no experience whatsoever in the area of wedding ceremonies. The Maori Apirana slips into one of Slütter's no longer quite so fresh white shirts and, mildly amusing, this, incorrectly hoists the Imperial flag to the jibboom. Then he shakes a bottle of champagne, grinning (as always, November has disappeared into the stokehold, Pandora somewhere onshore). Emma chews on a caramel and looks ten, oh, fine, *fifteen* years younger.

Lützow himself, in his prime, a touch too sure of himself, sparkles with electrical energy. It is quite clear and obvious, he remarks, that he has missed sophistication, the ritual of civilization, the crystal glasses, the creased white trousers, not so much as a thought for Kabakon, enough of that, it was an experiment, indeed a successful one, he can endure almost a year of asceticism, his various ailments are healed, but now back to Europe, to the Old World, whose complex attitudes are indeed quite conducive to locating oneself inside a structure into which one was born—of what use to anyone is escape if one does not return to apply what has been learned and experienced?

Give me your hand, darling. Away, far away. To Baden-Baden, Montecatini Terme, Évian-les-Bains—Queen of the Islands, we will visit Franz Liszt, Debussy in the summery freshness of France, then Berlin, Budapest, and the golden-hued opera houses of our ancient, ancient continent. We will buy an automobile, race toward Monaco with ecstatic, smooth speed, a tanned, unconquerable pair of lions, throw a thousand, nay, ten thousand marks on red, leave the winnings there so they will double and double again, then lobster thermidor, iced Pouilly-Fuissé, afterward an endless, vertiginous roundelay of strawberries, a whirling elfin dance under a Mediterranean half-moon.

Emma whispers her *I do*, Lützow of course does, too, Captain Slütter utters a few words he's half invented, half cobbled together, they are now man and wife, a champagne cork flies heavenward with a vehement pop. Apirana, his face, tattooed in concentric circles, hilariously wetted by the effervescent wine, fills up the readied glasses (his own fullest of all), empties his in one gulp, and, lured out of the reserved elegance of his people by the lightning-quick effect of the wine on his Maori cerebral cortex, he who has never drunk before, lovingly throws his arms around Lützow, Emma, Slütter.

This morning in Rabaul, the old *Prinz Waldemar* arrived as well. She is now anchoring, snow-white, stately, and somewhat piqued, directly next to what might be described as an extremely unattractive *Jeddah*, whose external appearance has not been particularly enhanced by the storm it sailed through in the Solomon Sea. People look over anyway, of course, at the captain and the bride and groom, wave hello, and Lützow in turn dashes toward the bulwark of the *Jeddah* in high spirits and, full of joyful anticipation of the elegant first-class salon of the *Waldemar* (for he has really had enough of sand fleas and discussions in the nude), climbs atop it quite recklessly, so as to leap over in a single bound from there onto the Imperial mail ship, all the while balancing two full champagne glasses like some comedic headwaiter and looking back toward the *Jeddah*, a witty remark, a burning cigarette dangling from his lips.

The sole of his shoe (which his feet are not used to wearing anymore) glances off the slippery outer hull of the *Waldemar*, he tries to reach the ship's rail, snatching, misses it, and now both legs are pulled upward, as if they were each hanging from two threads attached to the sky, he performs a salto (which here actually deserves its epithet *mortale*), then plummets headfirst into the harbor basin, into the water between the two ships, whose bilges, thanks to an unfortunately coursing wave or current, are drawing ever nearer to one another like two iron whales—and he is squashed by them. Not just legs and arms are pulped, but the whole Lützow.

After horrified cries, a red-striped life preserver is thrown down from the *Prinz Waldemar*, but it doesn't even make it to the surface of the water; instead, it gets stuck, futilely jammed between the two ships like a chewy bonbon between the tongue and the palate of a disinterested giant.

Emma, poised on the *Jeddah* in a yellowed wedding dress, not only witnesses the incident, but more or less has it imprinted in slow motion onto her retina, image by tumbling image; she sinks down on one knee in shock, as if in sudden prayer. Everything has happened so horribly fast. She raises a little embroidered linen cloth to the place on her upper lip where she has bitten herself, two tears well up, one each in her left and right eyes, the batiste is marked by a circular red stain. Slütter gently takes hold of her arm, lifting her up. She stands, fending off his hands, no shrieking, no further tears. Apirana's visage is a painted rock.

XIII

It seems to Slütter, who is sailing over to Kabakon to fulfill his murderous mission, as if Engelhardt were already expecting him, as if the former knew about the approaching executioner, as if Slütter were emitting a vibrating, throbbing force field. He has concluded that he will gird himself with a singular pitilessness, not in the least suspecting the extent to which Engelhardt has receded from the community of man and how easy it will be for him, on the other hand, to pull the revolver's trigger.

After having finished the work on the man-pits, Engelhardt had returned home and begun smearing black streaks all over the inner and outer walls of his house (and on the pages of perhaps a good dozen of his books) with pieces of charcoal, then he had sat down on the floor and proceeded to cut off the thumb of his right hand with the pair of scissors. Cauterizing the maimed hand with a flame, he had stored the severed thumb in a coconut shell filled with salt and walked outside and down the stairs onto the beach to wait for the arrival of the launch, the smoke of which had been visible on the horizon for a while now. It is low tide, it will likely rain soon, then again perhaps not.

Having just leapt from the launch, Slütter wades straight toward the beach through the almost hip-high sea, deliberately ignoring the little waves breaking on his back, although their force sends him stumbling once or twice. He has slung the revolver over his chest in a holster and forced himself into an automation of mind that prohibits him from seeing Engelhardt—sitting there in the sand, bearded, naked, shriveled—as a human being.

The latter raises his left hand in greeting (concealing the other, maimed one behind his back), suddenly recognizing Slütter as the man with whom he played chess one afternoon years ago (until the *solus rex*), the only person at that time who treated him with anything resembling respectful normality. Other faces now rise up before him abruptly, Hahl, Nagel, Govindarajan, Hellwig, Lützow, Mittenzwey, Halsey, Otto, Aueckens, every one of them eager to humiliate him, indeed, to destroy him with their diseased nature corroded with self-interest, and Engelhardt drops facedown into the sand, and he worships the visitor as if he, Engelhardt, were a Muhammadan bowing reverently toward Mecca.

He is so happy and thankful that that one honorable man is now seeking him out, yes, it's as if his magical effacement of Swedenborg's books had wrought this very miracle. With the nine fingers of his hands, he digs in the wet sand before him, despite the infernally tingling thumb stump; Slütter, yes, that was his name, *Captain* Slütter, absurd that Providence would send him this man of all people, he ardently hopes that Slütter has received his captain's license by now, that everything is squared away, as the sailor says, before it all goes to hell, haha, perhaps he even captains his own ship, he is tickled beyond all measure, alas, he cannot offer him anything, he has been living for, well, for how many years exactly?, quite exclusively off coconuts. (Can Slütter tell by looking at him that he's lying? No, that is completely impossible.) Groveling and with a wet, bleached beard, he lies there stretched out in the sandy ooze, his legs covered in the yellowish black bruises of leprosy, as if he had been repeatedly and cruelly beaten with blunt objects.

Slütter hastens to help him up and is shocked at his extremely light weight; it's as if he were holding a fragile little child in his arms or a dying old man whose skin feels leathery and brittle, like a lizard's. He notices that Engelhardt's ears stick out sharply from his skull, they, too, fragile and transparent, as if made of paper—and a strong feeling of pity overwhelms him. He puts his arm around Engelhardt's shoulders in support, accompanies him back to his house near the palm trees over there, and in doing so forgets that he has come to shoot him.

Twilit dimness reigns in the interior of the dwelling, thin rays of sunlight pierce through cracks in the wall, slicing every which way through the room. There is a coy stink of rotting fruit. Slütter, whose eyes only slowly grow accustomed to this, does not immediately see the young native boy sitting with a smile in the library on a rough-hewn chair. It is Makeli, who is playing with the scissors. Where are all these flies coming from? There are hundreds of them. Slütter is about to push open the drawn shutters as Engelhardt, mumbling incoherently, tampers with a bookshelf as if looking for something. Slütter pours a glass of water from an earthenware jug, sniffs it, grimaces, and puts it back down; the water exudes a putrid, moldy odor.

Tugging at his beard, Engelhardt begins to lament that not a living soul is working on the plantation anymore, these lazy simpletons have all returned to their villages, the ill-mannered Tolai chief has probably ordered that he be denied their service, after everything he's done for them, this is the thanks he gets, only young Makeli here has stayed with him, although he can't go back to his village anymore anyway since he's become a real German who speaks fluent German, they don't want him there anymore, and why would they, he most recently read him the second part of *Faust*, Poe, and even the harrowing ending of Ibsen's *Ghosts*. Engelhardt bursts into tears, he begins to twitch, his whole body is shaking. Makeli cannot help but sneer and puts his hands over his mouth. Slütter sees that the boy is missing a middle and an index finger.

The captain, who senses a vague but still distinctly immediate danger in the room, suggests they might go over and inspect the plantations, at which Engelhardt instantly ceases to cry and exclaims that this is an excellent idea, Makeli and Slütter ought to go ahead, nature will speak to them outside, he will come after them presently, he just has to nibble on something quickly since he feels so endlessly weak. Slütter and the native boy step out into the blinding sunlight.

Engelhardt really does want to explain himself to his guest, he wants to convey to him everything he has realized, really everything, but now the proper moment has passed. And so he keeps mumbling to himself, pacing back and forth in his dwelling: even Nietzsche ate his own excretions toward the end, after his breakdown in Turin, it's the great circle, the Mö-bius strip, the wheel of fire, the Kalachakra—only Nietzsche in his benightedness wasn't able to think the matter through to its conclusion, he never had to experience these continuous years of hunger; Engelhardt is here among unfortunate canni-bals who have evolved away from their natural, God-given instinct, dissuaded from it by the missionaries' blather, yet everything is actually so incredibly simple; it is not the coconut that is the actual sustenance of man, but man himself. The original man of the Golden Age lived off other men, ergo, the one who becomes godlike, the one who returns to Elysium re-fers to himself as: *God-eater. Devourer of God.* And Engelhardt reaches for the coconut shell wherein he has kept his severed thumb, carefully brushes off the salt, and bites into it, crunch-ing the bone to pieces with his teeth.

The tops of the palms sway, tousled and scruffy in the light wind of the afternoon. A bird of paradise trots back into the underbrush when it sees the two coming. Makeli shows Slütter the places where the coconuts were once harvested. Now of course no one cares about them anymore. It is a shame what's happening, but the mind-set, indeed, the unshakable attitude of his people is just like that. They simply leave everything where it lies, there is no responsibility, they are like children who grow weary of a toy. Slütter marvels at young Makeli, who has become German to such a degree that he judges his race as a colonial official might. And here, the coconuts, that's what Engel-hardt has been living off this whole time? Nothing else? And the young man?

Makeli smiles coyly. The bearded white man in his uni-form with the pistol is quite obviously not a bad man, not a monster as that Mr. Hobbes, in his *Leviathan*, showed man in general to be, but he is still an intruder, and like every intruder a danger. He, Makeli, drove away the musician, but it took a year, and he cannot wait so long for this one here.

Slütter walks over to a palm, touches its trunk, lost in thought, and looks out onto the ocean. He sees Engelhardt approaching from some distance. Slütter and Makeli are to come along, he, Engelhardt, has something interesting to show them in the jungle, he says, gesturing toward a clearing. They go in together, Engelhardt humming a cheerful melody and mincing before them—as his naked buttocks, reduced by malnourishment to something resembling cowpats, flap slackly back and forth—until they reach a spot that seems familiar to him; he drifts off to the left of the beaten path and indicates to Slütter that he ought to please walk in front. Makeli lets him by and begins to giggle uncontrollably.

Suspecting that he is in grave mortal danger, Slütter draws his revolver and declares that he has been sent to kill Engelhardt; they have, shall we say, grown weary of him over in the capital. But he has no intention whatsoever of doing it. Slütter points the revolver upward and shoots several times into the air. An earsplitting arpeggio of fluttering birds, complaining macaques, and hissing lizards fills the jungle. Engelhardt and Makeli stand frozen in place.

At this moment, Engelhardt sees twilight racing down upon him though it is still as bright as day. He sees the fading traces of the stars, he is standing on a wooded hill quite close to a city that has been abandoned for countless eons, the double moon rises orange-red and sallow on the horizon, that cozy little twin star of the *harmonia caelestis*; he believes himself to be in Arcadia and suddenly knows that his enigmatic vision has never been Kabakon, but the tapestry of his dreamworld, revolving and expanding into infinity. His certainty is the retching he feels in the face of his own birth. Highly developed species on other planets, he now knows, always behave like predators.

Engelhardt embraces his erstwhile murderer, kisses and caresses his hands, assuring him over and over again how thankful he is to him, something has now gotten sorted out in his head again, this wonderful clemency is an expression of cosmic destiny, indeed, his gratitude is an inexhaustible and immeasurable Fibonacci sequence. He's thrown out his Swedenborg, as a matter of fact. Crossed out and thrown out. Everything has to go. Bergson is the only one whom one might still be able to read, although he, too, has disqualified himself on account of his Judaism. And the cowardly order to murder him? Hahl probably gave it, Hahl being a Jew as well, he expected nothing else from this people, in all likelihood Hahl blackmailed him, hadn't he, Slütter should just admit as much, there's no shame in it, this sordid governor-philosopher is an insidious crook for whom every means is justified to see his disgusting aims achieved.

It's true, Engelhardt had unexpectedly turned into an anti-Semite; like most of his contemporaries, like all members of his race, he had sooner or later come to see in the existence of the Jews a scapegoat, tried and true, for each and every wrong suffered. The nervous breakdown wreaked on him by the leprosy had little to do with this; there was no causal correlation between his disease-induced irritability and that hatred of the Jews. Nonetheless, it blusters forth jauntily out of him: how

much blame the people of Moses had brought upon themselves in his eyes; the philosophical machinations by certain
charlatans that had made this or that mistaken path possible
in the first place; that there had been conspiracies against him
at the highest level, indeed, it was a Zionist plot that had been
hatched, the King of England was involved, Hahl, Queen
Emma (to whom he still owes a gigantic sum of money, he
recalls angrily), and others; that the whole miserable failure of
his blessed utopia could be chalked up to those who held the
reins in their greedy hands, those hands gnarled by Mammon
beyond all human recognition.

During this insane harangue by Engelhardt, young Makeli
creeps off unnoticed. He has had enough of the white men
and their lunacy and this island. Two fingers he's sacrificed,
and now he's had it. He wraps a cloth around his loins, points
the prow of one of the sailing canoes toward Rabaul, and as
he leaves Kabakon, he knows that it is forever, and he cannot
help but weep.

Slütter likewise turns his back on the furiously seething
Engelhardt, walks wordlessly to the beach, and marches back
out through the surging waves to the launch. He was unable
to kill the poor lunatic obsessed with the canard of a Jewish
global conspiracy, that's just the way it is, and Hahl will have
to swallow it, and if he intends to take Pandora away from
him, then Slütter can potentially offer him something else, his
own life perhaps.

But the girl is of course not behaving as Slütter would have
liked; as if he could just have frozen her in the everlasting
present, immutable until the end of all times. While Slütter is
on Kabakon, she remembers Apirana's offer on the *Jeddah* and

asks him if he will tattoo the story of the storm in pictures, he can do it however he wants, preferably on her back, there's lots of room there, and afterward Slütter can't do anything about it either way.

She takes off her dress and underwear and lays herself naked, facedown on the forecastle of the freighter, and as swallows dart up and down, high in the gloriously blue sky, Apirana prepares the traditional bone needles, gives her a piece of rope to bite down on, and begins to punch the tips dipped in black ink into the skin of the young girl's back.

As if he were a dark Pygmalion, he runs his skilled hand in rehearsal over the places he intends to draw menacing black clouds, gruesome krakens emerging from the troughs. The frigate birds that signaled the end of the hurricane will go on the right toward the shoulder, to the left down near the sacrum their little threatened ship, on it, in miniature, so tiny that they are barely perceptible, Pandora herself, Apirana, November, and Slütter. And finally, in the middle, between the shoulder blades trembling under his gentle touch, the storm itself: figment of a fantastic monstrosity from prehistoric times, baring sharp-edged teeth, writhing fiercely and tremendously, the monster scoops deluges of water from the ocean with its scaly paws to make the ill-fated *Jeddah* keel over.

When Slütter arrives back in Rabaul, the Maori's artwork is complete. Apirana has carefully dabbed off Pandora's bleeding back and bandaged it tightly with a bedsheet. Almost at the very same time, Makeli's little canoe sails into Blanche Bay. Observe now: events are coming thick and fast. Slütter encounters Hahl; the latter, being the *Realpolitiker* he is, has of course long since notified the English police that Pandora is in his custody ready to be picked up and taken back to Australia. To this treachery, Slütter can do nothing but add his own—having not killed Engelhardt—at which Hahl only shrugs, offers the captain a cigarette, and not without concision says that it's all rubbish now anyway, since there's threat of war—if he's understood correctly, a world war, as a matter of fact, in which enough disaster will rain down upon humanity, so it's quite honorable after all not to have partaken in Engelhardt's death, to boot.

To Slütter, in his contempt for mankind, this appears more than incredible, but he lets nothing show—he could still bring Pandora to safety, he could still keep her with him if only he maintained his calm. But the girl has long since made up her mind. This bearded, aging seaman is too forthright, too reliable for her; she feels his rage over the exquisite tattoo on her back to be petty-minded, his dreams (if he even has any) are not hers, he has grown as stale to her as the dropped toy has to the child. Yes, he has fulfilled his purpose, which fact she screams in his face standing on the landing pier, still barefoot.

Slütter takes leave of Pandora, and it tears apart his soul. In the distance, the cone of the purple volcano towers into the sky, and lizards conceal themselves timorously on its stony slopes. Makeli and Pandora, children of the South Seas, leave Rabaul together in a sailboat, headed into the unknown. The wind blows them to Hawaii, perhaps, or to the Marquesas, girded by vanilla vines, of which it is said their perfume can be smelled long before they are seen on the horizon, even all the way to Pitcairn, that volcanic rock in the empty, wordless south of the Pacific Ocean.

Engelhardt likewise becomes a child, a *rex solus*. Vegetative and simple, without memory, without foresight, he lives alone in the present; now and again receiving visitors, he talks incoherently; the people depart again and laugh about him: in the end he becomes an attraction for voyagers in the South Seas who visit him as one might a wild animal in the zoo.

In this time when simply nothing will happen while one awaits what is looming on the horizon, two German painters turn up in Rabaul: Messrs. Emil Nolde and Max Pechstein. Both have sworn off traditional modes of seeing and painting and feel themselves to be innovators of a hopelessly antiquated notion of art stuck in the previous century; yes, the French above all and their overly intellectual, spineless daubs are to be vanquished. Pechstein wears shorts every day.

They are passed around, the carousel of receptions and evening shows revolving. By day, Nolde mostly withdraws a few hundred yards into the nearby jungle to make a few sketches with vigorous and expressive strokes. Pechstein, growing bored, takes his leave and sails by steamship to Palau, while Nolde, when his cigars have finally run out, ferries over to Kabakon, since he's heard a deranged though quite harmless German is living there, leading the simple and quiet life of a naked native.

They get along as well as they can and talk about the future possibilities of art—Engelhardt moans his old litany that it is likely his fate to die without being understood, forgotten, without a trace. Nolde nods sympathetically, says the Jews are probably to blame for that, and following a sudden, strong impulse, asks if he might paint him in oils sitting on the beach beneath the orange-red evening clouds with a conch half raised like a horn in his thumbless hand: now Engelhardt truly has become a work of art.

The painting, admittedly, goes missing in the turmoil of the First World War, but fifteen years later, Nolde, who has now mentally fashioned himself into the first painter of the *Volk* for the new ruling powers, will recall the picture and make a sketch from memory and begin to paint the oil portrait of Engelhardt afresh using this drawing; this panel is produced without haste, elaborately, splendidly. It is perhaps, he says to himself, his finest work.

When it is done, he invites Gauleiter Hinrich Lohse over to his house in Seebüll for tea and rock candy. One assures the other of his mutual esteem, the artist leads the politician into his studio, and while Ada Nolde brings in a tray with aquavit and pilsner, Lohse inspects the work, uttering bumbling long drawnout oohs and ahs, sits down, stands back up, downs a glass of schnapps, walks around the easel while making a mental note to report the painter to the Reich Chamber of Culture as soon as possible. Nolde walks the slightly tipsy fellow to the door, there's a long and heartfelt handshake. After the Second World War, Lohse, who will become the Reichskommissar of Ostland and rule like a disgusting brute in Riga, Vilnius, Minsk, and Reval, will merely be denied his pension payments as punishment.

For years, Nolde has successfully schemed against the proscribed Pechstein, Tappert, Schmidt-Rottluff, Kirchner, Barlach, Weber—who naturally have greater talent at their disposal than he—but it's of no use; they impose a prohibition on his brush, too, clear out the museums, destroy a few pictures until it dawns on someone in the Reich Office for Foreign Trade how many Swiss francs they can get for these spatterings (essentially, so they say, vast expanses of color strung together in which one can occasionally recognize a mouth or a dog, sometimes a cloud, flowers, rarely a group of people—a child or an imbecile could paint like this), and so the paintings that haven't already been destroyed are sold off abroad. The second portrait of August Engelhardt goes to a private collector in Mexico City in whose house it hangs even now, over a sideboard on which freshly cut roses wither in a vase every day.

Nolde, who has propagandized against the Jews for as long as he can remember, and who is convinced his painting is the spearhead of a new Teutonic aesthetic, is unable to comprehend that his pictures are so unsuited to the new era. He falls into a deep depression, painting secretly, waiting, as so many opportunists of that time, until *finis germaniae.*

XIV

First, the student Gavrilo Princip, after hastily gobbling down a ham sandwich in Moritz Schiller's café, runs out into the street of that small, tranquil city in the Balkans and at point-blank range, pieces of sandwich still in his mouth, bread crumbs still on his sparse, downy mustache, fires right in the thick of things at the invidious despot and his wife Sophie with a gleaming revolver. Then, to put it mildly, one thing leads to another. The sea of flames that follows the murder sweeps across Europe with universal mercilessness; rickety planes buzz like paper dragonflies over Flemish trenches; anyone who's a soldier and possesses a mask scrambles, hands atremble, to yank it over his face as soon as the cry *Chlorine gas!* rings out; one of the millions of pieces of glowing shrapnel exploding on the Western Front bores like a white worm into the calf of the young private from the Sixth Royal Bavarian Reserve Division. Just a few inches higher, closer to the main artery, and it might never have come to pass that but a few decades later my grandparents would be walking apace in Hamburg's Moorweide, just as if they hadn't noticed those men, women, and children laden with suitcases loaded onto trains at Dammtor Station across the way and sent eastward, out to the edge of the imperium, as if they were already shadows now, already cindery smoke.

Patience, though. It is not like a distant thunderstorm whose fronts approach inexorably and menacingly—such that one can still get to safety—but rapidly and relentlessly and not without a certain drollery that the First World War comes to the Bismarck Archipelago, too. The Rabaul radio station that maintains contact with the German Reich via the Nauen Transmitter Station is shot up by an advance unit of Australian commandos and blown apart by several hand grenades thrown inside. The postmaster, who in former times had designed the labels for Engelhardt's coconut oil bottles, is wearing a uniform in the wrong place at the wrong time; an iron mail cabinet crashes down on top of him, and while falling, he is struck in the forehead by a soldier's bullet.

A few days later, an Australian battleship starts cruising around Blanche Bay, and a submarine surfaces. There's general confusion and great disorder; people flee to the governor's residence and barricade the windows by stacking chintz sofas and mattresses against them from the inside. Blond women who were just leafing through magazines and complaining about the putative recalcitrance of Malaysian employees sink to the floor in a swoon and must be tended to. The electricity goes out, the humming fans go silent. A lone shell fired off toward Rabaul by the battleship lands in front of one of the hotels with a buzzing wail, tearing a palm tree to tatters.

There ensues a kind of invasion, the course of which might be deemed quite anarchic. Chickens and pigs are rounded up;

artworks of infinitesimally small value are requisitioned and carried aboard ships to exhibit in Australian museums (even Hahl's reproduction of the *Isle of the Dead*); they arrest a soldier from Wagga Wagga who has raped a native woman and send him home in shackles as well; Hotel Director Hellwig wrings his hands at the great number of rude officers who drink his bar dry while boisterously singing "Waltzing Matilda"; driven from the jungle by the noise, a bird of paradise that strays into Rabaul is robbed, alive, of its feathers; soldiers stick the plume, the quill-end still bleeding, into their southwesters; after being dubbed Kaiser Wilhelm, the naked bird, screeching with pain, is kicked back and forth like a rugby ball amid snorting laughter; the crates of long-rancid coconut oil stored in the Forsayth trading post are opened with a crowbar; suspecting a cache of weapons, the soldiers merely find old-maidish bottles nestled in wood shavings; they cannot read the German labeling, uncork them in the hopes of booze, sniff them, and then, with theatrical expressions of disgust and noses pinched shut with thumb and forefinger, pour the contents out onto the sandy ground.

A detachment of Australian soldiers ultimately ends up on Kabakon, too. Engelhardt, who steps toward them on the beach, naked, amid the laughter of the uniformed men, is dispossessed forthwith. He is handed the sum of six pounds sterling for the run-down plantation, and it's left up to him whether to return to Germany. Six pounds for this life. He casts the puny sum of money at the Australian officer's feet, does an about-face, and vanishes into the shady jungle. He is not followed.

Captain Slütter, cruising with the *Jeddah* off Samoa in these confusing, peculiar times, reports to the commander of the SMS *Cormoran*, which is also lingering in the warm waters of the South Pacific; coal is in short supply, it is no longer safe to put to harbor anywhere, but they can't remain at sea, either, they are *sitting ducks*, as the British say. The crew of the *Cormoran* hopes for the expeditious arrival of the large German battleship *Scharnhorst*; in the meantime, Slütter, who has placed himself and his ship at the disposal of the *Cormoran*, is ordered to capture an unarmed French collier, recover the cargo, and torpedo the bugger.

And thus the aged *Jeddah* becomes a warship. She isn't allowed to hoist the colors of the German Imperial Navy, but Apirana, Slütter, and November do in fact manage to capsize the collier by affixing an explosive device to the prow of the *Jeddah*, setting a collision course, and escaping to safety with the tiny lifeboat just in time. The black plume of smoke can be seen for miles around. And so they bob, rowing off to the arranged meeting point with the *Cormoran*, which of course never appears. In its stead—it is nearly unbearable—two Australian warships show up; they take Slütter captive and land on a nameless island to collect water. Slütter is accused of piracy, stood against a palm tree, and executed. He acquiesces calmly, unshaven, refusing the blindfold. Another captive German sailor loans him his uniform coat so that Slütter doesn't have to die in civvies. When the bullets pierce him, he sees neither Pandora in his mind nor the soldiers aiming at him, just the solemn and distressingly unforgiving deep blue ocean. Cigarettes are distributed among the firing squad. The sailor's coat is returned after the sentence is carried out, and he wears it with head held high and a straight back; he will never sew up those four punctures at the height of his heart.

Escaping the soldiers by some ruse, Apirana, after long
odysseys that send him sailing over the inexhaustibly vast quilt
of the Pacific, that star field of his ancestors, and that blow the
fancies of white men out of his soul good and proper, joins the
New Zealand Navy on a whim. November, who had accompanied him, is swept overboard in a typhoon. He sinks with
open eyes miles down into the calm, night-blue cosmos of the
sea. Many decades later, Apirana will be the first Maori in the
New Zealand Parliament. He dies somewhere in midcentury,
ubiquitously honored, bearing a rank beyond reproach, as Sir
Apirana Turupa Ngata.

After having cheated their way around the Pacific for a long
while with extremely profitable cardsharping, the two crooks
Govindarajan and Mittenzwey are arrested on Samoa and de-
ported in chains to Australia on a prisoner convoy; the latter is
torpedoed en route by a German cruiser and sinks with all hands
into the surges of the Pacific Ocean.

Albert Hahl returns to a wintry, silent Berlin that is no longer quite so euphoric about the war, and there, over ten years—
using as a reference his card index filled with aperçus, diverse
discoveries, philosophical observations, and inventions—works
on his memoirs, which for want of an interested press remain
sadly unpublished. The helicopter Hahl envisioned, finally,
that he once dreamt up in a bright, flower-strewn kingdom by
the sea while observing the hovering flight of the hummingbird, will be developed much later, in the next war, as most
splendid inventions of humanity are products of its feuds.
Granted a halfhearted appanage by the Imperial Colonial Office, he devotes himself increasingly to private scholarship. As
politics irritate him, he writes the long letters of an aging man

who no longer occupies center stage. Even the philosopher Edmund Husserl receives mail from Albert Hahl, a densely inked, eighty-page epistle in which it is set forth that we men are living in a kind of highly complex motion picture or theatrical work, but suspect nothing because the illusion is so perfectly staged by the director. The letter is half skimmed by Husserl, dismissed as childish, and not dignified with a reply. Hahl—his hair has long since turned gray when the sun-crossed Führer of the Germans becomes swinishly insufferable—then conspires with the wife of Wilhelm Solf (erstwhile governor of German Samoa) by joining a resistance group whose brutish end on the piano-wire gallows of the imperium Hahl will not live to see.

Emma Forsayth-Lützow dies in Monte Carlo at the gambling table of the longed-for casino after placing her last ten-thousand-franc chip on the color red. Black 35 wins. She slumps down in her chair without a word, two gloved casino employees rush to fan air at her, a third brings her a glass of cognac that is spilled amid the commotion, leaving a dark stain on the bottle-green frieze of the gaming table, which will have vanished the next day. The Société des bains de mer de Monaco erects a headstone for her that reads *Emma, Reine des Mers du Sud*. Today the inscription is weathered but still quite decipherable.

XV

And our more-than-bewildered friend, our problem child? He does materialize once more, you know. Shortly after the end of the Second World War, in the Solomon Islands, on the battle-ravaged isle of Kolombangara, not far from the flattened peak of a smoking volcano, American naval units discover an ancient white man who is missing both thumbs living in a cave. He seems to have subsisted on nuts, grasses, and beetles. A young woman Navy doctor examines the old man, skeletally emaciated yet still oddly strong, and notes with great astonishment that he suffered for decades from a multibacillary form of leprosy, but that it has by some amazing miracle completely healed.

The long-haired graybeard is taken to and shown around a confusingly large military base on the island of Guadalcanal, which was wrested away from the Japanese. Wide-eyed, he sees everywhere friendly black GIs whose teeth, quite unlike his own ruinously rotten heap of dental wreckage, gleam with a secret, surreal luminosity; everyone appears so extraordinarily clean, their hair parted and clothes pressed; he is given a dark brown, sugary, rather tasty liquid to drink from a glass bottle slightly tapered in the middle; sedulous fighter planes set down on runways at minute intervals and take off again (the pilots smile, waving, from glass cockpits, radiant in the sunlight); with an expression of rapt attention, an officer holds a metal box with small perforations to his ear, from which enigmatic, heavily rhythmic, but still not at all unpleasant-sounding music emanates; the old man's hair and beard are combed; an immaculately white cotton collarless camisole is pulled over his head; he's given a wristwatch; they pat him gaily on the back; this is now the imperium; he is served a type of sausage brushed with garishly bright-colored sauce that lies in a bed of oblong bread as soft as a down pillow, as a result of which Engelhardt, for the first time in long over half a century, ingests a piece of animal flesh; here, a soldier of German extraction (his parents simply forgot their language of origin—it was assimilated *pars pro toto* into the *E Pluribus Unum*), one Lieutenant Kinnboot, in shirtsleeves, preparing with patient affability to ask Engelhardt dozens of questions for a newspaper, is mightily impressed when Engelhardt suddenly recalls the English language—which of course has grown somewhat rusty over the decades—and begins to speak, at first haltingly, then with increasing vivacity, of the age before the world war, no, not the one favorably just ended, but the one before that, even. And Kinnboot, quite riveted, lighting one cigarette after the other, forgetting to offer the bearded old man one, is unable to make notes anywhere but in the margins of a steno pad long since filled with scribbles, shakes his head again and again, and, smiling incredulously, he professes: *Sweet bejesus, that's one heck of a story,* and: *Just wait 'til Hollywood gets wind of this,* and: *You, sir, will be in pictures.*

And in fact, several years later—Engelhardt has now already left us—solemn, monumental orchestral music will surge before audiences. The director is present at the premiere, first-row seats; he is sitting there, biting at the crescent moon of the fingernail on his pinkie, chewing up the sharp keratin particles, the projector clatters, no, hundreds of projectors are flickering and beaming their cones of light, accompanied by wildly dancing dust motes, onto hundreds of screens, in Cincinnati, Los Angeles, Chicago, Miami, San Francisco, Boston, on which a white postal steamer, beneath long white clouds, is sailing through an endless ocean. The camera zooms in; a tooting, the ship's bell sounds the midday hour, and a dark-skinned extra (who will not appear again in the film) strides, gentle-footed and quiet, the length of the upper deck so as to wake with a circumspect squeeze of the shoulder those passengers who had drifted off to sleep again just after their lavish breakfast.

The author would like to thank Frauke Finsterwalder, Carol and Lars Korschen, Errol Tzrebinski, Angelika Schütz, Rafael Horzon, Humphrey Kithi, Ernst August of Hanover, and Frank Feremans for helping him write this book.